My name is Callum Ormond.
My brother is missing.
Our story begins . . .

MISSING

To Isobel

First American Edition 2013
Kane Miller, A Division of EDC Publishing

Text copyright © Gabrielle Lord, 2013
Cover design and internal graphics by Nicole Stofberg
Cover copyright © Scholastic Australia, 2013
Cover logo designed by Natalie Winter

First published by Scholastic Australia Pty Limited in 2013
This edition published under license from Scholastic Australia Pty Limited

Cover photography: Cal's head by Wendell Levi Teodoro (www.zeduce.org) ©
Scholastic Australia 2013; Cal's body © istockphoto.com/Sacha Bloor; lightning
© istockphoto.com/Leonid Tit; sky © istockphoto.com/Miroslav Georgijevic;
paraglider © istockphoto.com/Andrzej Burak; cliffs © istockphoto.com/Joakim
Leroy; stormy weather © istockphoto.com/o-che.
Internal photography and illustration: mobile phone on page 185 © istockphoto.
com/pressureUA; world map on page 185 © istockphoto.com/David Vernon;
skull on page 185 © istockphoto.com/zmina; tablet computer on page 155 ©
istockphoto.com/loops7; group playing volleyball on page 155 © istockphoto.
com/Eleonora Nazarova; girls playing volleyball on page 155 © istockphoto.com/
Iakov Filimonov; group playing guitar on beach on page 155 © istockphoto.com/
Kevin Klöpper; row of kayaks on page 155 © istockphoto.com/Laila Røberg;
tropical island beach on page 155 © istockphoto.com/Gergana Valcheva; map on
pages 146–145 and pages 046–045 © istockphoto.com/Eric Scafetta; icons on
pages 146–145 and pages 046–045 © photos.com/John Takai/art12321/Lumumba/
joingate; tag on page 049 © istockphoto.com/Robyn Mackenzie; mordred key
symbol on page 030 © istockphoto.com/Krystsina Birukova.

All rights reserved.
For information contact:
Kane Miller, A Division of EDC Publishing
PO Box 470663
Tulsa, OK 74147-0663
www.kanemiller.com
www.edcpub.com
www.usbornebooksandmore.com

Library of Congress Control Number: 2012952372

Printed and bound in the United States of America
1 2 3 4 5 6 7 8 9 10
ISBN: 978-1-61067-168-2

MISSING

GABRIELLE LORD

A DIVISION OF EDC PUBLISHING

DAY 1

90 days to go . . .

Home,
Flood Street, Richmond

11:04 pm

"What could it mean?" I remembered asking Boges, as the three of us stared at the image printed out on Winter's coffee table. "Piracy?"

"Something bad, dude," he'd said, "coming in 90 days."

"Why would they send it to me?"

Winter had looked up from the text I'd received earlier that day, pushing her dark hair back.

"You have quite a high profile these days, Cal," she'd said. "A lot of people have noticed you." She thought a moment before continuing, "Maybe it's some kind of warning, like the Drowner. We thought that note was a threat, too."

"The skull and crossbones image *has* historically been used both by pirates and as a warning symbol for other dangerous items," Boges had said. "The image of the world, however, makes me think this message could lean more towards piracy, due to the scope of the potential threat—it's not like someone's going to poison the whole world, for example. Well, I mean, that's unlikely. But piracy—attacking and stealing—that's more probable."

"Thank you, Professor Bodhan, for your enlightening lecture," Winter had smirked.

"In any case, the message is too vague to know for sure. Someone is toying with me again, and I'm sick of riddles," I'd snapped, suddenly tired of being used like a chess piece. A powerless pawn.

Despite Boges's best efforts, he hadn't been able to trace the sender.

That was this morning. Now, I looked out the window from my desk, trying to stop my mind from worrying. It was getting late and the house was breathlessly still. I was the only one awake, wasting my time trying to study. As if the strange message wasn't enough to take my mind off my already overdue physics assignment, almost a week had gone by since anyone had last seen Ryan and I was finding it impossible to concentrate.

Winter and I had gone around to his place earlier in the day. I picked up my wallet and fished out the small piece of paper that Ryan's mum had given us.

"He left it on his desk," Mrs. Spencer had said. "I'm really worried. Did he say anything to you?"

Winter had shaken her head. "I talked to him last week and he didn't say anything about going anywhere. What about you, Cal?" she'd asked, turning to me.

"He hasn't replied to any of the texts I sent him over the last few days," I'd replied.

I smoothed out the paper and read it for the hundredth time.

> Hi Mum,
> Don't worry about me. I'll be fine.
> I've made some really good new friends. They really understand me.
> I'll be in touch in a while. R

Winter and I had gone over and over the note, remembering a time when I'd been coerced into writing something just like it. By smudging some letters as a clue, my friends had figured out where I was being held. But this note was perfectly straightforward—no secret messages, no codes, no indication that it was trying to say something else. Ryan had just vanished somewhere with these new friends. Twins have an instinct about each other and my "Ryan alarm" was telling me something was wrong. I was having bad dreams again, which reminded me of the white toy dog nightmares that had plagued me before finding Ryan. Since then, Ryan had always told me everything . . . until now.

My study notes were spread all over my desk, but I wasn't taking anything in. My phone rang.

It was Winter. "I can't sleep. I'm thinking about Ryan."

"Me too," I said. "Wish I knew what's going on."

"You know, he did say he was always being mistaken for you and then when people realized he wasn't the famous Cal Ormond, they were disappointed. Maybe he was getting sick of it."

When we said good night a few minutes later, I thought more about what Winter had said. *Did Ryan resent being the Psycho Kid's twin brother?*

A sound on the street made me glance out my window, craning my neck to see what was going on. The noise came again, louder. It was the sound of a scuffle and someone crying out for help! As I stood up for a better look, a struggling woman came into view, being held by two strong-looking young men.

I took the stairs two at a time and within seconds I was out on the street, hoping to use surprise as my best weapon. I pounced on the bully closest to me, tearing him off the woman while grabbing her with all my strength to wrench her away from the two of them. She swung around, snarling—*did she think I was another attacker?* But then, quick as flash, her arm flew towards me, and as the two bullies laughed, she hit me with a stun gun.

I saw stars.

DAY 2

89 days to go . . .

UnKnown Location

1:45 am

I woke up and looked around, dazed. Where was I? I struggled to my feet, fearful and alarmed as the memories of the stun gun and the snarling woman flooded my mind. The whole thing had been a setup! But who were they? *What did they want?*

I looked around again. Dark walls were dimly lit by tiny pinpricks of light on the roof, like stars. There was no visible door and no windows. It was like being inside a cube of black glass. What was this place? I shoved my hand in my pocket to get my phone, then realized it was sitting on my desk back home. I groaned loudly.

I started banging on the walls. "Hey! Let me out of here! Let me out! Someone, help!" I was starting to get really scared now. I had no idea who these people were or what they were up to.

I tried yelling and screaming again, but it was no use. My voice simply bounced around the dark-black glass of the room. The thought that nobody knew where I was really terrified me.

How was I going to get out of here? Was this something to do with the bizarre text message? A flood of rage surged through my body. "You can't do this!" In the silence that followed my shrieking, it was clear that they could—and had. *What was I going to do?*

I noticed a table and chair in the corner. I went over and sat down, desperately trying to think. I didn't know what time it was or how long I'd been knocked out for. There was a numb, odd feeling where the stun gun had jabbed me.

I banged the table in anger and that's when I saw the pieces of metal there. I picked them up and turned the pieces over in my hands.

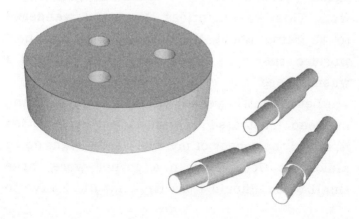

They looked like they might fit somewhere. But where? They must have a purpose. My anger died down as I fiddled with the bits of metal. The three long pieces screwed perfectly into the three holes in the metal disk. Now I had a kind of claw. Maybe I could smash my way out of here? But when I hit the glass with my metal claw, it just skidded along the polished surface. Not even a scratch. *Bulletproof glass?*

I went over the situation in my mind. I'd been grabbed, knocked out with a stun gun, and then put in this sealed room with these few bits of metal. Logically there had to be a way in and out, otherwise I couldn't be in here. I looked at the three prongs again. Maybe they went in somewhere? I started to look for three matching holes. I got down on my hands and knees and worked my way around the room. After a few minutes, I slumped against the wall. This was pointless. My mind wandered to thinking about Mum and Gabbi, and how worried they'd be when they woke up and I wasn't there.

"Let me out!" I yelled. But no one came. I hung my head, frustrated . . . and that's when I spotted it, out of the corner of my eye. There—right down almost at floor level in a corner—were three small holes. Should I try it? What did I have to lose? But what if it was a power outlet? What if putting this claw into the socket created a surge of electricity that would kill me? *Think, Cal, think*. That didn't make sense. If my abductors had wanted to kill me, they could have easily done so when I was knocked out.

Cautiously, holding my breath, I gently pushed the prongs into the socket and turned the disk, like a key, pulling my hand away as fast as I could. A whirring sound behind me was a door swinging open in the apparently seamless black mirrored glass. I hesitated for a moment. What lay beyond that door? All I could see was blackness. But I had to get out of there, so I bolted. Then I stopped. I was outside!

The night air was cool against my face as I spun around, ready to fight. But there was no one there—there was nothing but factory buildings. I was standing in the middle of a moonlit, deserted industrial estate. I looked back at the door I'd escaped through—there was no handle, and almost no sign a door was even there. The squat dark building that loomed behind me was disguised to look just like any other on the street.

There's something really weird going on. I've got to get out of here—fast. But as I started to jog away, I heard something coming around the corner towards me. I blinked, for a moment not believing what I saw—a cute fluffy toy puppy, trotting stiffly on short legs, wagging its tail, a powerful flashlight attached to its red collar. I watched, fascinated, as the mechanical puppy came up to me and stopped. It stood up on its back legs, cutely begging. I leaned down to pick it up, but the moment I touched it, I jumped back in alarm. The cute puppy instantly changed into a snarling beast—red eyes flashing, its sharp metal teeth gnashing at me!

Before I could recover from my shock, a harsh robotic voice said, "If you want to know what's going on, you have one chance to find out. One chance to find out what happened to Ryan. Here are your instructions. Point of Storm: 0300. I repeat, Point of Storm: 0300."

"What?" I asked, stupidly talking to the dog. "What's that supposed to mean?"

The robot dog suddenly switched off, its forelegs dropping to the ground. I stood alone among the silent dark buildings, the words echoing in my head. *Point of Storm: 0300.*

My head was whirling with confusion, but I knew I had to stay focused. What if this really was the key to finding out what had happened to Ryan? I couldn't let my brother down. 0300 sounded like the time on a 24-hour clock—three o'clock in the morning. Did I have to be somewhere by three? But where? And what time was it now?

I kicked the lifeless robot puppy at my feet. Frustrated and angry, I said out loud, "Where am I supposed to *be* at three o'clock in the morning?" to the locked and vacant factory buildings. As if in answer to my question, a car appeared in the distance. After what had happened to me, I was taking no chances. I ducked into a dark doorway as it approached. The words *Eagle Security* ran along the side of the small sedan. I made a quick decision and took a chance, stepping out into the dull glow of the streetlight. The car immediately stopped and a heavily built man in a blue uniform stepped out.

"What's your business here at this time of night?" he asked, his face severe. I thought fast— he'd never believe the truth.

"Wow," I said, "am I pleased to see you! Some friends of mine thought it would be funny to dump me out here and make me walk home."

"Are you carrying any identification? Any tools?"

"I've got my license," I said, pulling it out and opening it. "No tools." I'd broken *out* of a factory, not into one. Mr. Eagle Security studied the license, looking back at me. "I know your name for some reason," he said. "Ah, I know—*The X Factor*, right?"

"Not bad," I said. "I'd really appreciate a ride to a main road so I can get home. Can you tell me what time it is?"

"It's after two in the morning," he said, glancing at his watch. "So let's get you out of here, Mr. Famous."

Moments later we were heading for the highway. All the while, my head was spinning, trying to think what *Point of Storm* might mean. It was a puzzle. Just like the pieces of metal had been a puzzle. Whoever was behind all this was offering me a sporting chance—if I could just figure things out.

Mr. Eagle Security told me he had another large factory complex to check out a bit further down the highway. As we traveled, I looked for familiar places, my eyes desperately searching for buildings or street names I recognized. I scanned signposts as we flashed past them. We were heading south when I saw a signpost pointing back the other way—*Dolphin Point, 10 m.* Now I knew where I was—about twelve miles from home. I was about to ask the security guard to drop me off when the name on another sign jolted me. "Hey! Stop the car!" I yelled. "That's the turnoff to my place!"

The car pulled over to the edge of the road and I jumped out. "Thanks a lot," I said. "It would have been a long walk home."

"You've still got another four miles to go," said the security guard.

"I'm a runner," I said. "I'll be home in twenty-five minutes."

The sound of his car faded away as I put my head down and started to run the four miles to Storm Point.

Storm Point

2:58 am

Storm Point turned out to be a tiny fishing village, clustered on the headland, with one dimly lit main road running along the length of a rocky inlet where waves crashed and broke noisily. Opposite, a handful of shops were scattered along the waterfront, but everything was dark and locked at this hour.

I'd made it. *What now?*

I spotted a light at the end of the jetty that reached out into the sea. Puffing hard, I loped along, getting my wind back. As I came closer, I saw that the light was coming from a motor launch moored at the end of the jetty, heaving on the swell. Was Ryan being held in there?

I was about to start moving stealthily towards the boat when I yelped in shock as I was taken down again from behind. My pent-up fury exploded.

"Who are you? Why are you doing this to me? Where's my brother?"

My assailants made no response.

"Hey, I know you! You're the three thugs who attacked me earlier! What's going on? Answer me!!"

No one answered. In total silence, and despite my constant struggling, the three of them —the same two guys and the snarling woman— held me tight and started putting scuba gear on me!

I kicked and shouted and made it as hard as I could for the silent attackers, but it was useless. Within a minute, I had the weight of a scuba unit on my back. Kicking and struggling, yelling out, I was dragged onto the boat, which started speeding away from the jetty. A diving mask was roughly pulled over my face as a heavy weight belt was attached around my waist. My protests were ignored as a regulator was shoved in my mouth, fins were pushed on my feet and I was hauled on the gunwale and tipped backwards into the cold, black water!

I sank like a stone as my arms flailed wildly, surrounded by wet darkness, the only sounds the hissing of the oxygen tank and my own gasping breath. I struggled to stop my panic rising as I sank through the murky deep. *Calm down, these guys are not trying to kill you. There's something else going on.* My job now was to make sure I survived to find out what that was.

I felt my feet scrape the seabed. Time to get out of here! The first thing I had to do was ditch the weight belt. I couldn't be more than a half a mile out from Storm Point and once I got to the surface, I could also get rid of the heavy tank on my back and swim to shore.

I groped around until I found the weight belt release catch. I pressed it and felt it drop away. I began to push my way to the surface when someone crashed into me from behind and as I clambered to break free, I felt the air flow to my mouthpiece stop.

They'd switched off my air supply!

Desperately I twisted and turned, but my hands couldn't reach the valve. I was going to drown! Fear swamped me as I frantically pulled the useless regulator out of my mouth. How much air did I have left in my lungs? I spun wildly in all directions. I looked up and saw a faint glow above me. The moon! Could I make it to the surface in time? I kicked off from the bottom, swimming as fast and as hard as I could.

I felt the weight of the water pressing down on me and forced myself to blow out slowly as I came up to avoid getting the bends. My lungs were screaming for oxygen and my heart was hammering in my chest.

I kept striking upwards, kicking fiercely, as the moon shone brighter through the water. I spotted a darker patch—the boat! I had to get away from them. That last assault on me had been murderous. Now I was convinced whoever these people were, they *were* trying to kill me. I don't know why they'd toyed with me before, giving me chances to figure things out. I broke the surface as quietly as I could, swimming slowly to minimize splashing, but it was no use, a blinding light shone straight into my eyes. I'd been seen by my enemies! As I squeezed my eyes against the glare, I could hear my name being called. Somebody was cheering! What the . . ?

"Hey, Cal! Come aboard! You've done really well. Come and get warm!"

The light shifted from my face, shining a path to the boat. There I could see the three people who had attacked me waiting, calling out to me. Were these people *crazy?*

"It's OK. Come on up and we'll explain everything. We'll tell you what we know about Ryan. Everything will make sense, we promise."

"No way!" I shouted back. "I'd rather swim home!"

"Come on, Cal," called out the woman. "We were just testing you. And you've passed! Please trust me. Don't you see now that everything you've gone through tonight was carefully planned? Come on board and you'll see."

My teeth were chattering with cold by now. I desperately wanted to get out of the freezing water, but could I trust this gang?

Wary, I swam over to the launch, ready to take off at the slightest whiff of more danger. The three of them were lined up along the side of the boat, as I swam nearer.

"Passed with flying colors," said one of the young guys, who was wearing a wetsuit. "And don't worry, buddy. I'd never have let you drown."

Now he tells me, I thought, angry.

I let them help me up over the side of the boat where a small barbecue was sizzling. "OK," I said, pulling off the swim fins and slamming them down on the deck. "I want some answers. Who are you? What's going on?"

"Take it easy, Cal," said the woman, flinging back her thick tawny braid and putting a hand out.

"Take it easy?" I yelled, pushing her hand away. "Last time I saw you, you stuck a stun gun into me and I woke up in some kind of prison cell."

"That was regrettable," she agreed. "But we had to meet you somehow."

"How about asking? A phone call, maybe?"

"That wouldn't have worked at all," she said, seeming to pay no attention to my sarcastic tone. "My name's D'Merrick."

I remained standing, still very cautious.

"It was impressive," D'Merrick continued, "how quickly you put the key together and got out of the room."

"Nicely done," added the young guy in the wetsuit, reaching out his hand. "I'm Axel. No hard feelings, I hope?"

"And I'm Paddy," said the second guy, also extending his hand, a hamburger in the other.

"Not sure if I'm ready to shake hands with any of you," I said. "I've just been through a nightmare because of you people."

"Maybe a hamburger will help," said Axel. "And hot coffee and an explanation." Under the light on the boat I could see that he was a strongly built man with close-cropped dark hair and a cheeky grin—which I could have done without right now.

"You switched off my air supply!" I snapped.

"And waited right behind you, making sure you didn't panic yourself into trouble." He passed me a hamburger wrapped in a paper towel. "Go on," he laughed, "it's not poisoned! Wrap yourself around this and D'Merrick, our team leader, will explain what's going on."

Cautiously, I allowed myself to relax a little, sitting down opposite them and taking a bite of my hamburger. I was ravenous and wolfed the rest of it as D'Merrick spoke.

"We're from SI-6—Secret Intelligence, Special Branch. We work as a unit within NIS, the National Intelligence Services, and we've had our eye on you for a while. We liked the way you handled yourself when you were on the run for that whole year, and how you solved the mystery of the Ormond Singularity. And now you've passed the tests we put you through. You used your intelligence to figure out how to get out of that sealed room." She pulled her thick braid around to the front as she continued, "And you figured out the instructions Fido gave you."

"You set up that dog?" I asked.

"That's right," said Paddy, folding his thick arms across his broad chest. "We thought we'd use something different to get your attention, courtesy of our robotics section."

"And you kept it together in an extreme situation—when Axel stopped your oxygen. All pretty impressive, Cal."

I'd finished the hamburger and I was speechless. This had all been a series of *tests*?

"I've heard enough—you said you knew about Ryan. Tell me! Where is he?"

"That's where you come in," said D'Merrick.

"Me? I'm asking about Ryan."

The three of them looked at each other. "Look, this might sound tough to you, but we're not cleared to talk about that just yet."

"Not cleared?"

"Once we get back to headquarters," said D'Merrick, "we can explain everything. In the meantime, just relax, get warm and we'll get you there."

The powerful motor launch took off, heading north. My three new acquaintances kept busy around the boat until we docked at a private jetty somewhere south of the city, where a black car was waiting for us. I was still very reluctant to go anywhere with them. D'Merrick opened the car door for me and said, "Just trust us a little longer—I know it might be hard after what you've been through, but believe me it will be worth it— especially when you know if Ryan is safe."

That clinched the deal. I climbed into the back of the car and even dozed off as Paddy drove and Axel and D'Merrick made small talk.

I woke up with a jolt when the car stopped.

My guts tightened in apprehension and fear as I saw we were back outside the building where my ordeal had begun.

"It's OK, Cal. This time you're our guest," said Paddy. Hesitantly, I climbed out, staring at the mirrored doors of the main entrance. As we approached, the doors swung open and the four of us walked through. I heard the doors quickly and quietly lock behind us.

Clayton Morris Industrial Estate, Palmers East

4:37 am

We were in a foyer with elevators straight ahead and corridors running to the left and the right. Paddy and Axel peeled off into the right-hand corridor while D'Merrick indicated I should follow her down the left-hand hallway. About halfway down, D'Merrick ducked through a door on our left as a small noise made me stop. I started to look around, but a huge force brought me down to the floor as someone grabbed me by the throat and began to choke the life out of me.

Extreme rage exploded through me. *I've had enough!*

A massive surge of anger enabled me to pivot the pair of us around so that I was on top instead. As we swung around, my elbow found the soft part of his stomach and I dug in with all my fury. He let go of my throat and I instantly pinned his arms down with my body weight. His twisted face was now far too close to mine. But it wasn't twisted in pain. The guy was smiling at me—a broad smile showing very white teeth.

The smile became even broader as he said, "Well done! I was told to take you by surprise and you beat me. No hard feelings, I hope?"

My jaw dropped. "You mean this was another one of their tests?" I yelled.

He grinned. "The name's Max. Are you going to let me get up now?"

My burning rage had subsided, but I was still seething with anger. These people had no right to treat me like some lab rat. I jumped up and threw open the door through which D'Merrick had vanished. She looked up in surprise from behind a desk.

"I've had enough of this! I'm going to the police. I don't care if you are SI-6, MI5 or the whole of the KGB put together! I'm sick of being pushed around, kidnapped, practically drowned and then set upon by your trained gorilla out there! I demand that you let me out of here!"

"Sorry about that," said Paddy, who had come into the room behind me. "We wanted to see how you'd do when you thought nothing else was going to happen—when you were relaxed and unsuspecting. But you handled it well."

"Then handle *this!* I'm outta here!" I yelled, pushing past him and heading for the door.

"You're free to go, Cal, of course," Paddy called after me. "But if you go now, you won't find out what's happened to Ryan or where he is. You sure you really want to leave?"

I stood, conflicted, at the doorway.

"We wouldn't have put you through all those tests without a very good reason. Think about it. Think about your brother."

I turned and looked down the corridor to see a tall, broad-shouldered man coming towards us. Something about him exuded an air of authority, and as he approached, I could see his shrewd, direct gaze under thick eyebrows. He put out his hand to greet me and almost without hesitation I responded, shaking his hand.

"Good to meet you at last, Cal," he said. "I'm Benedict Bellamy—but everyone here calls me BB." He looked me straight in the eye and said, "We'd like you to work with us."

Work with them? Is that what all of this had been about? I was being recruited by an intelligence organization? But that didn't make any sense.

"Why don't you come back and sit down," said Paddy, "and listen to what BB has to say? After you've heard him out, then decide. If you still want to leave, I'll show you to the door and that'll be the end of it. OK?"

I grudgingly acknowledged that I had nothing to lose by hearing what BB had to say, so with my anger fading, I went back into the room and warily sat on a chair next to the others while BB stood up leaning against the desk, one leg crossed over the other in front of him.

"Cal," he started, "I'll tell you the whole story. A girl—someone I know very well, or thought I did—has gone missing. Our intelligence reveals that she's almost certainly gone to Shadow Island. You might have heard of it?"

I shook my head and BB continued, "Shadow Island is a resort—a retreat for young adults. They call themselves the Paradise People and it's run by a man called Jeff Thoroughgood. Thoroughgood seems to be a good guy—he's done a lot of work with street kids and running youth refuges. He helps get kids back into either education or employment. He now runs Shadow Island, a family property, as a rest and recreation center for kids who need to get away from it all. I'm telling you all this because when we discovered the possible whereabouts of this young girl, we found out that your twin brother, Ryan, has joined the Paradise People."

"Ryan?" I said in surprise. "On Shadow Island? Why would he be there?"

"I was hoping you might have some ideas about that," said BB, running a hand through his thick hair.

"I guess he hasn't been quite himself for a while," I said, remembering. "What sort of a place is this rest and recreation island?"

"It's a combination of vacation activities and a retreat center—with a strong self-development curriculum for teenagers. Physical activities, self-defense and motivational classes, that sort of thing."

Ryan had mentioned meeting interesting new friends. They must have been Paradise People.

BB continued, "We can't send an agent because they'd be too old. That's another reason why we thought of you. But sending you in publicly might attract too much attention since you're so well known. We want you to go there covertly—no one would know you're on the island—and gather intelligence for us. We really must be very discreet about this."

There was a silence in the room while I considered what BB was suggesting. I knew he was right about going undercover. Ryan wouldn't thank me for turning up and taking the spotlight with his new friends.

"I should mention that we have some concerns, Cal," BB said finally. "We've recently heard rumors about the place, and that's the other reason we want to get an operative on the island."

"Rumors?" I frowned. "What kind?"

"A few months ago, Jeff was taken ill and left to recuperate in Switzerland. Since then, his brother Damien has been running the island. So as well as seeing if the girl is there and is OK, we'd like you to have a look around and make sure that everything is as it should be at the resort."

"We're concerned that the group might not be what it seems," said D'Merrick, leaning in her chair so that her braid swung forwards. "There was a girl who came off the island recently who said some odd things about the place. A worker from the Bank Street Youth Center alerted authorities to the possibility of an issue, but there wasn't enough evidence to go in officially to investigate. Apparently some kids are coming back mixed up, and others aren't returning at all."

"Do you think the Paradise People and their new leader might be taking money from these kids?" I asked.

"We don't think it's that," BB replied. "Going to the resort doesn't cost anything."

There's no such thing as a free lunch, I remembered hearing my dad say.

"But we are worried that somehow the kids there might not be being well taken care of," BB continued. "Before you make a decision, Cal, you need to know a couple of things. This is a personal mission—it's something we're doing 'off the books.' Which means that we give you supplies and get you there, but we can only offer limited help once you're on the island. We'll give you a satellite phone with a line direct to me so you can contact us if necessary. Just in case something goes wrong. This has to be a completely secret operation—no one else involved."

"What do you think is going to happen? It's just a bunch of kids on a tropical island," I said, puzzled.

"I'm sure everything will be fine," said BB, "but things can often turn out . . . unexpectedly."

I noticed that BB and the other three were all looking intently at me. I thought about Ryan, and my mind was made up. "OK," I said, hoping my voice sounded controlled and calm. "I understand. But there are a couple of things *you* need to understand before I agree to this. I have two good friends, you probably know who they are—Bodhan Michalko and Winter Frey. I'll do this for you, but only on the condition that I can talk freely to them, and Ryan, and have their help if it ever becomes necessary. I've trusted them with my life before and they've never let me down. And one other thing, no more surprise attacks, thanks. I'm over those. That's the deal. Otherwise, I'm walking out of here."

Now it was BB's turn to stop and think. Finally, he nodded and pulled out a folder and opened it, bringing out a photograph and placing it in front of me. He'd accepted my terms. "This is the girl you're looking for. Her name is Sophie."

I picked up the photograph and studied it. It was of a pretty, smiling girl of about sixteen or seventeen. She had striking dark-blue eyes and blond hair pulled back in a high ponytail, with freckles across her nose.

"You'll need to observe her and make sure she is all right—all the time staying undercover. Later, we might consider seeing if we can get her home again." I went to hand the photograph back to him, but he shook his head. "Keep it," he said. "I've got plenty more." He must have noticed my puzzled look because he continued speaking. "Her full name is Sophie Ann Bellamy. Sophie is my youngest daughter."

Now I noticed the deep concern and worry in his

eyes. "We won't send you over there unprepared, Cal. Paddy will organize the necessary training and equipment for you."

I suddenly remembered my physics assignment. "What about school? And my mum and Gabbi?"

"You can leave that to us. We'll talk to your family for you," said BB. "You have enough to focus on."

I thought of something else. "Did anyone from SI-6 recently send me a text message? A picture of the world with a skull and crossbones on it?"

The blank look on BB's face answered my question. "Skull and crossbones?"

"Never mind. Someone sent me some random picture."

"Maybe it was a prank. From a friend?"

"Maybe. So, how am I going to get there?" I asked, changing the subject. "Airplane? Boat?"

"We'll talk about that later," said BB. "Shadow Island presents a few challenges—especially for a covert insertion."

Winter's House
Mansfield Way, Dolphin Point

6:49 pm

"Covert insertion, dude?" said Boges. The three of us sat around Winter's kitchen table as I repeated what BB had said. "That is serious military talk. That's *commando* talk."

I'd told them everything that had happened with SI-6 and Benedict Bellamy—the insane tests they'd put me through the night before, then the revelation that they knew where Ryan was and that they needed my help. I pulled out the photograph of BB's daughter.

"She looks young," said Boges, picking up Sophie's photograph.

"I wonder what BB meant by 'challenges' on the island?" Winter said, helping herself to another cookie.

"I don't know yet. But it seems that there have been rumors about the Paradise People and the guy who's running it now. They think he might not have the same kind of experience as his brother. Someone at the Bank Street Youth Center had some concerns."

"Bank Street?" Winter asked. "I've done volunteering at that center. I know Rebecca, the woman who runs the place. We should ask her what she's heard."

Boges pulled out his tablet and within moments had found what he was looking for. "Check this out, guys. This is the Paradise People Resort website."

WHO WE ARE
THINGS TO DO
THE ISLAND
CONTACT US
SEARCH

Feeling lonely? Misunderstood?
Need time to get your head sorted out?
Come join us on Shadow Island.

We offer fun adventures, campfire talks and physical
activities that will develop your character and give
you the confidence to deal with life's challenges.

Limited to ages sixteen to eighteen.
Meals and accommodation included.

ALL YOU NEED TO BRING IS YOURSELF!

Boges clicked on "Things to Do" and zoomed in on the pictures on his screen so that we could all see it—kids playing volleyball on a beautiful beach with a vivid blue sky above. There was a row of palm trees and a big mango tree, with kayaks underneath, in front of a sparkling ocean. Table tennis games were happening on the grassy area beside the beach.

"I feel like going there myself," said Winter. "It looks fantastic. I could handle a bit of tropical island right now."

"What is it, Boges?" I asked, noticing the two lines on his forehead coming together. "You're wearing your 'something's-not-quite-right face.'"

"Because something's not quite right, dude. Who's paying for all this?"

"I thought about that, too. It's some kind of charity, I guess," I said. "So that's it, guys," I continued. "I go there undercover and check that Sophie and Ryan are both OK. And have a bit of a look around and make sure everything is above board—that the guy who's running the place knows what he's doing and hasn't gone troppo."

"What's that?" asked Winter.

"When too much tropical heat makes people go crazy," Boges explained.

"Doesn't sound like you'll need us at all,"

sighed Winter, scrolling through the website and admiring the photographs. "Unless you need a ball boy or girl to jump into the surf and bring back a lost volleyball."

"Great work if you can get it," said Boges. "And you've got it, dude."

"Paradise," I said, rubbing it in a bit. "What could possibly go wrong?"

DAY 4

87 days to go . . .

Bank Street Youth Center

2:15 pm

The three of us walked into the youth center—a converted church hall with a small cafe area on one side, battered old couches and armchairs, and a couple of computers.

Winter went ahead of us to the small office. A young woman looked up and smiled, getting out from behind her desk. "Hi, Winter. How are you?"

"Good thanks, Rebecca. These are my friends Cal, and Boges," she introduced us.

"Hi, guys," said Rebecca. "Haven't noticed you two around here before."

"We wondered if we could talk to you about Shadow Island," I said, leaning against the back of an old couch.

"Are you thinking of going there?" Rebecca asked cautiously.

"Why? Is there a problem?"

"I'm not sure," she said, frowning. "It's just that I know someone who was there for quite a few months—Brittany Philips. At first, she was very happy. She loved it there and started helping out, and was really pleased when they asked her to stay on as a staff member. But by the time she got back, she was in a terrible state. She'd been asked to leave and she wouldn't, or couldn't, talk about why. She was always a bit on the quiet side, but after that she was really timid and withdrawn. She bunked here for a couple of nights, too scared to leave the premises."

"What was she frightened of?" I asked.

"She didn't say," said Rebecca. "It might all have been in her imagination. She had an anxiety problem, and nightmares too. I heard her yelling out about a key or something." Rebecca paused, trying to remember. "I'm sure that was it. She was raving in her sleep about a key, and when I woke her up she mumbled, 'If they know I know, I'll be in terrible danger.'"

I looked questioningly at the others. "*If they know I know*—what? About a key? And who's *they*?"

"Search me, dude," Boges said.

Winter shrugged her shoulders. "What do you think she meant, Rebecca?" she asked.

"I wish I knew. I shook her awake because she was so distressed. But then she just clammed up. She wouldn't tell me anything more. Now I don't know where she is and I worry about her. And there have been other kids too. I've noticed that some of our most neglected and vulnerable kids are the ones who end up being drawn to the place. Most of them come back after a few weeks. But a couple of the kids, I've never seen again."

"They might just be getting on with their lives," Boges suggested.

Rebecca didn't look convinced. "Could be. I've just got a bad feeling about that place."

Later, as we walked back to Winter's house, it felt like Rebecca's bad feelings were contagious. Shadow Island had changed from being a tropical paradise into something potentially much more sinister. Even the name now sounded menacing. And what was the key for?

"What did you make of what Rebecca said?" Winter asked me.

"Not sure yet," I said. "I was thinking about Brittany Philips and her nightmares."

"I don't like the idea that some kids seem to be missing," said Winter. "Shouldn't the police be doing something?"

"What can they do?" asked Boges. "At that age, kids can leave home and go where they like. They might just have gone off and not told anyone."

That was true, I knew. And surely, if there'd been any real problems, the authorities would have been asked to investigate Shadow Island by now. Rumors are just that—a game of whispers. Lots of kids "disappear" for a while. I know I did for a whole year. Although, I mused, I wouldn't wish that kind of life on anyone.

Winter interrupted my thoughts saying, "You know Cal, until I met you, Boges and Ryan, and then Harriet, I might have been one of those vulnerable kids. I might have been the sort who went to Shadow Island and then just—just . . . "

". . . disappeared?" I laughed. "No way. I can't imagine that! But I think we need to talk to Brittany Philips," I said.

"We've gotta find her first, Cal," Winter reminded me.

DAY 8
83 days to go . . .

SI-6 Headquarters,
Clayton Morris Industrial Estate

10:02 am

"OK," said BB, standing in front of us and pointing to the screen on the wall. Axel, Paddy, D'Merrick and I sat around a long table, ready for my briefing. I had been eager to learn more in the last few days, but SI-6 seemed to be running on their own schedule. Perhaps this was the downside of an "off the books" operation.

"This is Shadow Island," BB announced, "as per the Paradise People's website. It's quite small—about four miles long and a couple of miles wide. Like most of these islands, it has steep volcanic cliffs and dangerous ocean breaks on the windward side, with a more sheltered bay on the leeward eastern side."

BB pointed to the screen and continued, "There've been small rumbles from a volcano there, but very little recent activity, apart from the occasional tremor. The terrain is rugged and mountainous in the middle, with one heavily forested large peak that's usually covered in cloud. This area," BB pointed to the screen, "was used for a while as a penal colony in the 19th century. Parts of an old stone prison and the prison governor's residence are still there, but they're all derelict now. The island was also used by the military during the Pacific War."

BB turned back from the screen to face us. "Jeffrey Thoroughgood has been running the place as a youth camp for a number of years now. As you can see, it's a pretty, tropical island—but like all paradises, it has its serpents too. There are potential dangers on Shadow Island, like the Gympie Gympie trees which grow in the rainforest areas which cover much of the island. It's a harmless-looking tree with heart-shaped leaves, but if you brush up against it you'll be in pain for months. There's also a nasty climbing palm called a 'Wait-a-while,' which has hundreds of little hooks along the stems. Bump into that, and you'll be there for quite a while getting unhooked."

"Great place for a retreat!" I said. It looked like I was going to be busy dodging danger—not playing volleyball.

RESORT

WELCOME TO
**SHADOW
ISLAND**

BB went on, "For many months of the year, the surrounding water is dangerous due to the strong currents and huge seas on the windward side, which makes the western side of the island almost inaccessible. There are also large colonies of Irukandji jellyfish. Have you heard of them?"

I had and I didn't like the sound of those suckers. "Aren't they the ones that are even more deadly than box jellyfish? Plus they're tiny and almost invisible?"

BB nodded. *Great.*

BB hit a button and a tiny, glassy creature with long, vein-like threads drifting behind it, pulsed across the screen. "Anyone who goes swimming must wear a stinger suit. Jeffrey Thoroughgood has them stored in the resort."

Paradise is getting better and better by the minute, I thought, as I stared at the image on the screen.

"So you must take care to avoid these hazards. I'll make sure there's an adrenaline shot in your first-aid kit, Cal, just in case you need to take action against anaphylactic shock," BB said. "That can happen if you get enough toxin to make your body go into meltdown. It can be fatal if not reversed quickly. Paddy or Axel will show you how to use the shot. OK?"

He looked at me. "Any questions?"

"Have you heard anything about some kind of key on the island?"

BB frowned. "I don't think so. Why do you ask?" It was clear from the puzzled look on his face that he hadn't. I decided to let Boges and Winter fill in SI-6 on Brittany Philips later, so I moved on to my next question. "How will I get on the island?"

I saw the four of them looking at each other before BB spoke. "Obviously going by sea is out of the question. Any craft would be smashed to pieces on the rocks on one side of the island, and on the other side, a beach landing could be easily spotted."

"Parachute?" I asked.

"Paraglider. We notice you've used a hang-glider before. The plan is to fly you most of the way at night, when the weather conditions are just right, and then you will glide in for a quiet landing on Shadow Island. But we'll make sure you get enough training and practice jumps in first."

"All right, that all sounds OK."

BB's face became concerned and thoughtful. "Cal, I want you to think carefully about this. This is the sort of job that should rightly be done by an experienced operative with commando training. We don't anticipate problems with the Paradise People themselves, but to a large degree you'll be going into an unknown situation. Do you understand what I'm saying?"

In the silence that followed BB's words, I thought about it. A mysterious group of people and a night landing on a small island in the middle of a huge black ocean. A killer surf and jagged rocks on one side, possible volcanic activity and stinging trees in the middle, and deadly invisible jellyfish all around? How could I resist?

"Right," I said. "When do we start?"

11:14 am

Paddy and BB accompanied me downstairs to the equipment area of the Special Intelligence building, where I was given a strong backpack with lightweight camping gear and army-style rations, as well as a secure cell phone, with built-in encryption capabilities. Paddy explained how to use all its specialized applications.

"I've included a solar phone charger. Might be useful when you're camped out in the jungle," Paddy said.

"You'll also take a small satellite phone," added BB. "You might need it in case you can't get a phone signal. But the secure channel can only be accessed at eleven o'clock at night and only for a few minutes. I don't want to expose this mission to anyone else in SI-6. This job is strictly under the radar. Your call sign will be Night Hawk. Mine will be Condor. OK?"

BB wished me luck, shook my hand and left. The worry in his eyes was easy to see. I realized that I was keen to help reunite Sophie and her father. For a moment, I felt a pang of sadness for my own. But I shook it off as I tried to focus on Paddy's instructions about my new equipment.

DAY 11

80 days to go . . .

Home
Flood Street, Richmond

7:22 pm

The next few days I spent getting used to jumping
out of a helicopter under the watchful eye of an
instructor. When Mum asked me where I'd been,
I just said I'd been flying. It wasn't completely
untrue. If she'd known the whole truth, she
wouldn't have been very happy. There are some
things mothers are better off not knowing.

I was relieved when I heard Ryan had finally
been in touch with his mum and reassured her
he was on Shadow Island and having a good
time. I'd be even more relieved when I'd seen
him myself to confirm that was really true.

I marveled at how persuasive SI-6 must have
been about my upcoming absence because no one
seemed to have any problem with me taking off
for a "special apprenticeship" at a conveniently

concocted elite flying school. I really must get these guys to help me out next time I have an assignment due, I decided.

"When are you going to take me up with you, Cal?" Gabbi asked, looking up at me with her big eyes as I put some clean dishes away.

"Soon, piglet," I said, ruffling her hair.

"Don't call me that!" she said, kicking me.

"Hey, no kicking! How about the way you demolished that tub of ice cream?" I joked, as Gabbi threw a dish towel at my head.

DAY 16

75 days to go . . .

Disused Airfield, Finchley

8:13 pm

My backpack was packed and I was ready to go. Earlier in the afternoon, Winter and Boges had said goodbye.

"Good luck," Winter said, giving me a fierce hug. "And while you're away, we're going to track down Brittany Philips. We need to know why she was made to leave the Paradise People Resort. *And* why she became so anxious and frightened."

That weighed heavily on my mind, and I knew I'd be relieved once Winter and Boges found out what Brittany knew.

"Later, dude," said Boges, giving me a punch in the arm. "Don't go troppo or get all James Bond on us, OK?" he smirked.

"You know me, super low-key!" I joked back.

Now, I watched as the pilot ran through his pre-flight checks. I was anxious to get going, frustrated by the bad weather which had delayed my departure to the island.

BB pulled something small out of his pocket. "There's a false bottom to your backpack—it's waterproofed and secure. Put this inside it," he said, handing me a small USB stick. "On it is something we've developed called the Stealth Hacker. It's two programs in one—the first hacks into a system and collects information, then the second removes all traces of the hack. I just thought it might come in handy," he smiled. "I was a Scout a long time ago and 'be prepared' is a good motto. The casing is waterproof and shockproof so it's pretty indestructible."

As I slipped it into the secret compartment of my bag, I thought, *Boges would love this.*

Night Flight

10:45 pm

It felt like we'd hardly spent any time in the air when we began to descend and I prepared myself for the jump from the helicopter.

The instructor gave me the thumbs up—*go!*

I hesitated for a second, staring down into the vast blackness of the night. Then, wishing myself luck, I tumbled out, dropping like a stone with the rushing air taking my breath away, as my hands grappled with the controls. As I leveled out, I felt the glider wing fill with wind and arch over me.

The sound of the helicopter receded and now all I could hear was the wind rushing against my face and the crazy banging of my heart as I swayed through the night sky. Ahead of me, I could see my target. The pilot had pointed out the island to me as we approached and I steered the paraglider by the couple of lights that shone in the distance below, pinpoints in the ocean of blackness.

Soon my vision adjusted. I could see the island better—a darker black than the ocean surrounding it, the mountain in the middle rising up to meet me.

The wind had picked up and buffeted me back and forth. I was going fast now and I braked, frantically steering away from the jagged rocks and steep cliffs I knew were on this western side of the island. If I crashed onto those, I'd be torn to pieces in the wild surf!

I leaned to the right, turning from the churning dimness of the water and the invisible rocks, flying over treetops, coming in lower, looking for a suitable landing spot. I needed some sort of cleared area. I sure didn't want to crash-land into vegetation where I might fall into a Gympie Gympie tree.

As I continued to pull on the brake loops, I noticed a clearing among the trees, about the size of a soccer field. In fact, it *was* a soccer field—I could now see the goals at either end. A perfect place to land. I tacked, turning into the wind, to prepare for a landing.

Four or five yards above the ground, I got ready, bending my knees, legs together, then braking. Remembering my training, I took some long running strides until my legs touched the ground. And then I was down, safely back on solid earth again. It would have been nice if I'd had an audience to appreciate my near-perfect landing. But on this occasion, an audience was the last thing I wanted. I hoped no one had noticed my illicit flight. As quickly as I could, I gathered up my equipment, folding it hastily. I hurried from the field, taking off the harness as I went.

I looked around for a place to hide my gear. The area was almost like a jungle, halfway up the mountainside. Not far from where I was standing, a huge Norfolk pine tree that had crashed down years ago had created a long "wall" from its huge girth. Its massive trunk lay in front of me, wrapped in overgrown vines and with small saplings springing up around it. I shoved the paraglider gear into a hollow under the fallen tree and rearranged vines and twisted creepers over the top.

Part one of my mission was accomplished—I had landed safely on Shadow Island. Now all I had to do was find Sophie and Ryan, make sure that they were both well and safe, hang around for a little while to check out what was going on, then I could contact BB and be out of here in a matter of days. I was keen to see Ryan, but also a bit anxious—why had he felt the need to come out here? Was it because of me? Or was there something else going on with him that I didn't know about?

I unrolled my sleeping bag and finding a sheltered spot alongside the giant tree, spread the ground sheet and made myself comfortable behind a curtain of vines and leafy undergrowth. I'd grab some sleep now and at first light I'd make my way down to the resort.

DAY 17

74 days to go . . .

Shadow Island

5:53 am

I woke to the sound of the first bird calls in the pre-dawn. Strange birds whooped and whistled, twittered and sang. Everything felt misty and damp. I pulled out a cereal bar for breakfast and started to make my way down the mountain, heading for the lights of the resort. The buildings were set back some distance from the beach on the opposite side of the island. The dawn wasn't far away, but it was still dark under the tall canopy trees and I was glad to find a path of sorts, roughly cut out of the jungle growth. I used the flashlight from my backpack, keeping the narrow beam down and trained on the ground. I didn't want to be seen and blow my undercover presence on the island as soon as I'd arrived.

As I approached the outer buildings, some instinct made me stop. While I stood there, checking out the resort in the distance, there was a strange rattling sound and a crash. For a moment, I thought the noise was from the coconuts I spotted falling from the trees. But they weren't the reason for the rattling and shivering in the trees around me. The ground was jolting! With a shock, I realized it was an earthquake! I waited, but nothing more happened. The coconuts stopped falling. The birds started calling again. The earth was still once more.

I listened. I could hear something, a slight rustling of the leaves, and the sound of steady movement. Thankfully it wasn't footsteps—this was a continuous sound, almost like a low hiss. I could see movement on the path ahead and I swung the flashlight beam in front of me.

Immediately, I jumped back in alarm! Caught in the intense glare of the flashlight, the beady eyes of a swaying python stared coldly into mine as it dangled from a tree branch right in front of me. The snake had to be at least six feet long, with mottled skin and yellow eyes.

Don't run, don't make any sudden movements. My heart hammering in my chest, I cautiously backed away, slowly changing direction, moving sideways into the undergrowth away from the creature. But no matter where I went, those beady eyes remained fixed on me, the reptile's head turning with every move I made. I'd never been scoped out by a snake like this and it was very unnerving. After I'd gone a little deeper through the undergrowth, I shone the light back through the leaves and saw those eyes still staring after me.

Taking long, deep breaths to calm myself, I continued my descent, but now very carefully watching where I put my feet and flashing the light quickly ahead of me in case there were more snakes hanging around. For all I knew, the one I'd just encountered came from a big family.

Almost there, I paused and checked the contents of my backpack, making sure both phones and the charger were safely hidden under the false bottom. I pulled out the USB with SI-6's Stealth Hacker program on it, ensuring it was safe in the pocket of my pants. From now on, I would keep it with me at all times, just in case an opportunity arose for me to download information about the resort or the Paradise People.

I was thinking about how to find Ryan when a voice called out, "Is there someone there? Identify yourself! Say the password!"

Quickly, I crouched down, taking cover behind a clump of bushes. A password? BB hadn't mentioned anything like that.

I peered around the leaves and saw a young

man in a loud Hawaiian shirt and white shorts standing by what I saw now was a fence. Looking around, I realized the buildings were ringed by a tall security mesh with barbed wire running along the top. Inside, bright flags flew and huts painted in bright holiday colors contrasted with the fence running around them. What a fantastic place, I thought, taking in the beautiful beach huts, the basketball courts, and hearing the soft roar of the surf only a little distance away. But what was with the fence? Who were they trying to keep out? Or keep in? Perhaps the security fence was to keep the pythons out?

The man turned and looked straight at me. He started hurrying in my direction. If I broke cover and ran, he'd see me for sure. But if I stayed, my chances weren't much better. As he came closer, I saw that he was actually looking past me. I remained frozen where I was, barely breathing. I didn't dare look to see what had attracted his attention.

Behind me, I heard someone crashing through the jungle, running away back up the mountain.

"Hey! Come back!" the man in the Hawaiian shirt yelled. But whoever was running away kept going. The man looked undecided, unsure whether to chase whoever it was, or remain at the fence. Eventually, he must have decided to give up the pursuit and he moved away, head down, using a two-way radio, aiming towards the corner where the fence made a right angle.

I was puzzled. Who was the runner? And why would you run away from the Paradise People Resort?

I remained crouched down for a while, thinking that it was going to be tougher to get to Sophie and Ryan than I'd expected.

7:25 am

By now, the sun had risen out of the sea, after turning the sky gold and pink. Through the fence, I could see what looked like dormitory buildings with clotheslines alongside, and beyond them, I caught glimpses of a swimming pool, surrounded by tall palm trees decorated with twinkling lights. A blue-and-gold flag with a cross of white stars billowed on a tall flagpole. Beneath it a smaller dark pennant fluttered.

From somewhere in the resort, the smell of a delicious breakfast teased me, reminding me how hungry I still was. I jumped as a loudspeaker broke the silence. "Breakfast is served!"

I saw people in friendly groups laughing and talking as they made their way towards a long, block-like building that I guessed was the dining hall. Others with beach towels and swimsuits ran through the grounds, heading for an early morning swim. I could hear the joyful cries and yells of teenagers as they splashed in the sparkling swimming pool. But I didn't have time to admire the attractions of the island resort—I was on a mission and needed to stay focused.

My attention was caught by the red door of one of the nearby dormitory buildings opening and three people walked outside, laughing. I could hardly believe my eyes when I saw that one of them was Ryan! He looked well and happy as he laughed and joked with his companions. But as they turned away, Ryan's expression changed. Not much, but enough for his twin brother to spot it. His face had gone from happy to I'm-not-sure-about-this, the same expression I had when I was worried about something. He seemed to be limping, too. Maybe that's what was causing the face, I thought. He's injured himself in some activity and is putting a brave face on it.

There was no sign of any staff now so I ducked over to the mesh fence, calling from the outside as loudly as I dared. "Hey! Ryan! It's me!"

My brother stopped in his tracks. I saw his face register complete disbelief, then astonishment, then a worried smile. He hobbled over to join me on his side of the wire.

"Cal!" he frowned. "How come? What are *you* doing here?"

"It's a long story. But I'm really pleased to see you—we've been worried about you. The way you just took off. What happened to your leg?"

Ryan looked around behind him, checking that no one was watching.

"That's a long story too. And yeah, I did just take off. I had my reasons. We can talk about that later. But we can't talk here. The CCTV cameras might pick this up." He sighed. "See those boats over there?" He pointed to a couple of kayaks lying upside down outside the corner of the fence. "I'll meet you there after breakfast, before roll call."

"Roll call? That sounds like school," I said.

"They do it two times a day for safety reasons. But I think it's to make sure everyone is where they should be. I'll be done in half an hour or so, OK?"

"I'll be there," I said. "There's a password."

"That's right. They change them every now and then. The current one is Hannibal. Not sure why they have them. The counselors— the people in the Hawaiian shirts—keep an eye on everyone and help out. Mostly they're pretty cool. But that guy over there? The groundskeeper?" Ryan pointed to a thin guy with black hair slicked back from a narrow face. "That's Elmore. Watch out for him—there's definitely something off about him."

Ryan must have noticed the look on my face. "I know it sounds weird, but there's a lot about this place that just doesn't add up. Some of the other kids told me if you're somewhere you shouldn't be, you have to stay out of security camera range. If Elmore spots you, you get called up to Damien's office. Damien says it's because he has 'a duty of care' for us—he's responsible for us and needs to know where we are at all times, like good parents do. Look. I've gotta go. You'd better get lost, too." He looked around and I saw teenagers coming out of their dormitories, all heading down towards the breakfast room. The smells were unbearably tempting.

"Mmm. Something smells good—sausages?"

"They have great cooks here," Ryan explained, "I'll give them that!"

"Grab some food for me, please, Ryan?" I asked, my mouth watering at the thought.

We parted, Ryan to join a small group of chattering girls, while I headed back to the undergrowth where I hid myself, watching the proceedings. The Paradise People and the resort here sounded different from any resort I'd ever heard about. It looked like a whole heap of fun. But what sort of resort has roll call? And something was going on here that had caused Brittany Philips to have nightmares. Maybe she was just the sort of person who couldn't really cope with being away from home. But she had said some weird things and maybe there was something more sinister involved. And that's exactly what I was here to find out.

Breakfast was over and I was about to sneak over to the trees by the kayaks, when I heard someone calling, "Ryan! Ryan!"

I turned around, thinking someone was calling out to my brother, but then I saw that the counselor was yelling at me—I'd been spotted! Then it dawned on me. The counselor thought *I* was Ryan!

As casually as I could, I strolled over towards him. I saw now that he was only a little older than me and very well-built, as if he'd been working out a lot. He was wearing another of the crazy Hawaiian shirts, this one covered with yellow pineapples. I noticed it had *Paradise People Resort* embroidered on one of the chest pockets and his fair hair was flattened down under a baseball cap decorated with the intertwined *PPR*.

"What are you doing outside? You should be having breakfast," he said, his eyes suspicious. "Password, please."

"Hannibal," I said confidently.

"And you haven't answered my question," the counselor said.

"I don't have to answer to you," I said, feeling defiant to this guy. Who did he think he was?

"Ryan, you know the rules around here."

What was this place, I wondered, a detention center?

I thought quickly. "I was told to check the kayaks," I said vaguely. "Make sure they're ready for anyone who wants to use them later."

The counselor looked puzzled. "Who told you that? The boss?"

"Yep. That's right." I didn't want this conversation to go any further so I turned and started walking away.

But the counselor hadn't finished with me. "I've been watching you, Ryan. And I don't like your attitude. I'm not sure if you've got the right team spirit. You'd better not be late for roll call. You've already got one black mark against your name."

I kept walking away, giving him a wave as if to acknowledge what he had just said. But my mind was in turmoil. What kind of a resort was this, with overzealous counselors, a nosy groundskeeper and passwords and black marks?

I risked a backward glance to see that he was

still staring suspiciously after me. I prayed that Ryan was safely eating breakfast and would stay out of sight until I could do the same.

7:48 am

Once the counselor had left, I stopped fiddling with the kayaks and snuck off into the jungle. As I looked for a way through, I skidded to a halt in front of a large tree with heart-shaped leaves—it was the Gympie Gympie stinging tree! Phew, that was close, I thought, looking at the prickly little barbs covering the plant and making a mental note of its position.

I turned to walk away and promptly stumbled into something stuck in the ground. It was a headstone. I looked down and saw *Solomon Foote 1818–1842* carved into the leaning tombstone.

"Oops. Sorry, Solomon," I whispered, scrambling back. I'd ended up in an almost-overgrown clearing set back from the beach. It must have been a cemetery for the convicts from years ago. It was fairly small—I counted around thirty to forty headstones scattered around. It was a peaceful place and I settled down nearby to keep the resort compound under surveillance, nestled down in some leaves to stay hidden.

From here, I could hear the yells and shouts of kids surfing and others playing a fierce game of volleyball further along the beach. It wasn't long before I saw my brother hurrying in my direction, limping slightly, looking behind him as he came. I whistled to him and within moments, he had ducked down beside me.

I gave him a brotherly hug, but Ryan pulled away. "Here, I brought you some food," he said, handing over sausages and some squashed rolls he'd smuggled out of the dining room.

"Thanks, bro," I said carefully. Clearly he was upset about something.

"So what *are* you doing here? Checking up on me?" Ryan asked abruptly.

I started to explain why I was there and how I'd arrived. Ryan was suspicious at first, but eventually, he was satisfied.

"Are you OK?" I asked, finishing the last sausage. "Tell me what's been happening."

"Like I said, something weird is going on here. At first, I didn't notice. I was so stoked at all the activities and the cool campfires on the beach at night. But then—" he shrugged before continuing, "things just didn't feel right."

I told him about when I thought the first counselor had spotted me. "But it wasn't me he was after, it was someone else behind me running away through the jungle up the mountainside. Do you know who it was?" I asked.

"Might have been one of the kids who are hiding up in the jungle. They break in and steal food sometimes. And they raid the supply boat when it arrives. I don't know who they are for sure. I heard Damien say that there were some hot-headed kids that came here quite a few months ago—they didn't fit in and were really aggressive so he asked them to leave. But they refused and ran off. Damien's been looking for them since then."

"They just live in the jungle, do they?"

"Apparently. I haven't been here long enough to really find out. None of the new people know anything about them and the ones who have been here for a while won't say."

I thought of Rebecca and what she'd told us about Brittany and her nightmares. "Have you heard anything about some kind of key?"

Ryan shook his head. "But, whoever these missing kids are, they aren't the only mystery around here. I think some others have disappeared. One day they're at roll call, then the next, I don't see them anymore."

"They probably just go home. What's weird about that?"

"But there's no way off the island except for the supply ship, and that only comes once a fortnight to bring supplies and transfer people on and off the island. Apart from that there's only Damien's submersible. And I'm talking about kids just vanishing between roll calls, on days when there's no ship."

This sounded bad. What if Sophie had disappeared?

"And did you know there are snakes in there?" I pointed to the jungle around us. "I had a run-in with one on the way down from the mountain."

"Yeah, the pythons. Damien has warned us about them. He says they're too small to be a danger to humans, and to just watch where we're going."

"The one I saw didn't seem so small!" I said, remembering those eyes and long scaly body. "Any other ideas about what happens to these kids?" I asked, my concern deepening.

"Well, I noticed one guy being escorted into the office building the other day—Damien's study is in there and it's strictly out of bounds. He didn't show up at evening roll call that night. I wanted to know what happened to him. That's how I did this." He pulled down the thick sock above his sneaker to show me a bandage. "I sprained it when I came off the roof," he said.

"You jumped off a roof? Is that why you're limping?" I asked.

"I was eavesdropping, but I didn't hear

anything—and then I lost my footing and I fell and twisted my ankle. I was really lucky nobody saw me. I told everyone I'd hurt it playing volleyball on the beach."

"How many kids have disappeared?" I asked.

"He's the third one I've noticed. I asked other people and they said not to worry about it. Damien says sometimes kids get news from home and have to be taken off the island quickly. And in that case, they're taken in the submersible. Then they don't have to wait for the supply ship. But Cal, I don't believe him. Because I saw one of the disappeared kids—the one I'd spotted being escorted into Damien's office. He *hadn't* left the island."

"Why don't you just ask him what happened?"

"I couldn't. I saw him running as if he was late for something, but he was running away from the resort. I took off after him, but I couldn't catch him because of my ankle. And then—he just kind of disappeared near the mountainside."

"You mean you lost him?"

Ryan shook his head. "I didn't lose him. He lost me. One moment he was running through the jungle. Next minute he was gone—right into thin air."

"Not possible, bro. He must have gone someplace."

"I searched everywhere. I had to be really

careful because there was a big clump of Gympie Gympie trees near where I saw him vanish."

"Maybe he fell down a mine shaft or something."

"There aren't any mine shafts here. This is all just tropical rainforest and volcanic rock. I looked everywhere. Then I made the mistake of mentioning it to one of the counselors. He reported me for being out of bounds. That guy's been on my case for a while."

That explained the counselor's comment to me about my poor attitude when he thought I was Ryan.

Ryan winced as he went to get up. "What is it?" I asked.

"It's my ankle. The nurse in the first-aid office told me it's a bad sprain and to keep off it. Instead, I've been running around after disappearing kids. It's getting worse."

I had another look at his ankle and could see the swollen flesh around the bandage. "You've got to rest that," I said. A plan was forming in my mind. It was bold, but I hoped it just might work. "Ryan, listen to me. You can't keep going on this—" I indicated his injured ankle. "But I can. How about I take your place? We swap clothes, and nobody will know the difference. That way, I can start investigating this place as well as making contact with Sophie."

"Sophie Bellamy?"

"You know her?"

"Yeah, she's a really nice girl. She's had a tough time at home. We've talked a couple of times. I think she likes me."

I grinned and punched his arm and Ryan couldn't help smiling. Then I became serious again.

"Well? What do you think of the changing places idea?" I could see that Ryan wasn't one hundred percent happy about it. "Look," I said, "I know it looks like me coming on the scene and taking over. But it's not like that. It makes sense, Ryan. You're out of action with that ankle. Think about it."

Eventually, Ryan said with a sigh, "I guess you're right. I go into hiding and you take over my life here?"

"I'm just standing in for you—while you're injured. I'm not taking over your life."

He stood up, and tried to put some weight on his injured foot. "Argh!"

"Come on. Put your arm around me and I'll help you up to higher ground and find a good hide-out for you. I'll give you my binoculars and you can keep an eye out for anything suspicious. You might even get to spot one of the runaways and find out what on earth is going on."

As we made our way through the jungle and

up the sloping mountain side, Ryan briefed me about the daily routine of the resort. "Morning call is at seven, with showers and breakfast, and then roll call at eight thirty. There are general activities till lunchtime and then free time in the afternoon. They've got movies and computer games in the recreation center, plus meditation and self-esteem classes. Outside there's rock climbing, swimming, surfing and water sports, but you need stinger suits to go in the water. You're not allowed to go around to the western side of the island," said Ryan, "because of the dangerous surf breaking over the jagged rocks. And by the way, we're out of bounds right now. Did you notice those orange flags on the side of the path?"

I had, but I hadn't paid much attention to them.

"We're not meant to go higher than the flags—because of the pythons and the Gympie Gympie trees. And the runaways. At least that's what they tell us. I think Damien is a bit of a control freak."

We'd reached the massive fallen tree trunk against which I'd stowed my gear. Ryan and I scouted around and found a better hiding place for him—a scooped-out overhang in the rock, behind a curtain of jungle vines. I gave him my emergency provisions, my binoculars and camping gear.

"How are we going to keep in contact?" I asked as I went to leave.

"Phones are handed in to Damien's office while we're here," Ryan said. Then he grinned, pulling his phone out. "I kept mine. But you'll have to be careful and keep yours hidden too."

I paused, not sure how to ask the next question. "So, bro . . . you never did explain why you came here in the first place?" I asked quietly.

Ryan's face clouded over and he was silent for a long moment. "Let's not get into that now, we've got bigger things to think about first."

"Fair enough, another time," I said. Pushing him seemed like a bad idea. I started to head off back down the mountain. "Hey, Ryan?" I added. "You didn't send me a weird text message with a map and skull and crossbones, did you?"

"No. Got some new pirate friends, have you?" Ryan joked.

"Worth a shot," I shrugged, turning to leave.

"Cal!" Ryan called out after me. "Remember to limp!"

8:19 am

As I hurried down the mountain, I was really starting to wonder about this place. Ryan had mentioned so many odd things—kids disappearing, runaways who raided for food, counselors who acted like guards.

Caught up in my thoughts, I didn't notice the palm frond sticking out over the rough track. I jerked back as my jacket was caught by a dozen sharp little hooks. I'd walked straight into a Wait-a-while palm! I tried pulling away, but only succeeded in getting more entangled. It took me ages, and a couple of painful jabs to my fingers, before I finally freed myself from all the hooks.

As I neared the resort complex, I noticed a group of bodysurfers running back from the beach and I hurried to join them, remembering to limp a little, managing to get through the compound gate before it closed behind us. Everyone was milling around happily. Maybe Ryan always stood with the same people. I hesitated, looking around, when the girl from BB's photograph ran over to me and grabbed my hand—Sophie Bellamy.

"Ryan! There you are! I thought you were going to be late again."

Great, I thought. I'd passed the first test.

Sophie dragged me over to stand beside her near the front of a raised stage area. I glanced around. There were about forty of us, with perhaps slightly more boys than girls.

And now the boss arrived, stepping up onto the platform, a folder in his hand. So this was Damien Thoroughgood. He stood well over six feet tall, broad-shouldered with a dignified air and dressed in khaki shirt and pants, his hair cropped short. His white teeth flashed when he smiled, and he smiled a lot. He greeted us and then started to read out the names in alphabetical order. When it came to "Ryan Ormond," I answered like the rest of them—"I'm here." He lifted his head from the folder and fixed me with a penetrating gaze. I felt my heart start to race. Had he noticed something? I saw his eyes narrow. Was my mission going to come undone even before it had started? I braced myself.

"How's that ankle coming along, Ryan? You feeling all right?"

Slowly, I let out the breath I'd been holding in. "It's OK," I said, wondering if I was supposed to say "Sir" or something else.

Thoroughgood nodded and then passed on to the next name. Finally we were excused, but as we started to move away, Damien looked my way and beckoned me over. "Good to see that ankle's getting better. Have you given any more thought to the matter we discussed the other day?"

Problem. How was I going to answer that? I tried to look like I was contemplating something.

"I need your answer fairly soon, Ryan," Damien said. "Otherwise you might miss out. So what's it to be?"

I didn't have a clue what he was talking about, but I had to give some kind of answer. "I'm still thinking about it," I said, nodding, hoping I looked like I was deep in thought.

"Good. That shows you're someone who doesn't rush into things. But I also need people who can act decisively."

"You'll have your answer very soon," I said. *Just as soon as I find out from Ryan what this is all about!*

That seemed to satisfy him and he strode away, taking a phone call on the way back to the office building.

8:41 am

When I was certain there was nobody in the bathroom, I went into a stall and closed the door, pulling my phone out. I called Ryan, keeping my voice as low as possible. "Thoroughgood just asked me if I had an answer for him, he asked you about something. What was it?"

"I forgot to tell you, sorry! He invited me to join The Edge—it's like an exclusive adventure program."

"OK, that doesn't sound too bad," I said.

"But you're not allowed to talk about it," said Ryan. "No one must know that you've been invited. And that seems suss to me. Why would you have to keep that a secret?"

"Maybe he thinks other kids might get jealous, or feel hurt if they're not included?"

Footsteps approached the bathroom from outside. "Gotta go," I said, hanging up.

2:14 pm

I joined in some activities for the rest of the morning, spending a bit of time with Sophie Bellamy—not too much in case she figured out I wasn't Ryan—just enough to get to know her a little. A couple of times I caught her looking at me oddly.

"Your ankle seems to have gotten better really quickly," she said.

"It comes and goes a bit," I said vaguely. Actually, I was having a bit too much fun and I'd forgotten to limp enough. *Idiot*, I scolded myself.

"Seems to have gone quite a lot," she said, giving me an enquiring look. "And there's something else. You seem—I don't know . . . "

"Come on," I said, not liking the direction of the conversation. "Do you feel like a swim?"

The rest of the time, I dutifully watched with

my "sprained" ankle as most kids went wind-surfing or rock climbing. Damien had organized team sports with Dean, the counselor who'd been so suspicious about me at the fence earlier. He seemed to be Damien's second-in-command.

At lunchtime, I'd managed to stash some food in my backpack for Ryan. Afterwards, I watched a game of soccer, resisting the temptation to join in. Sophie saw me on the sidelines and came over to me.

"Hey, Ryan! Wanna watch that movie you mentioned yesterday?"

"I–I forgot which one you mean," I said lamely.

"The one you were going to get out of the DVD library. You were raving about it!"

"I never told you what a bad memory I have, did I? I'm really sorry. Let's go and choose something else. Your pick this time."

"OK," she said slowly. "Come over to the library and we can watch it this afternoon."

"Man, I'm sorry. I can't do that. There's something else I need to do."

"Need to do? Like what? Collect seashells?" she joked.

"It's something personal," I said.

Sophie gave me a puzzled look. "What is it with you? I thought we were going to be friends, but now I'm not so sure."

She walked away without a word, heading for the girls' dormitory. I wanted to call out to her, but thought better of it. I needed to head to Ryan's hide-out, deliver my food package to him, check his ankle and be back in time for evening roll call. I glanced at my watch. It had been a really hot, tropical day, but now clouds were piling up and it looked like we might be in for a storm later in the evening.

I felt bad about the conversation with Sophie and how I'd gotten off to a shaky start with her. Maybe Ryan could give me some tips about recent conversations so that I wouldn't put my foot in it so much.

I waited until Dean had turned the corner of the tall fence and disappeared before I walked off away from the resort compound, heading for the out-of-bounds flags.

As I neared the flags, a voice yelled behind me. "Hey! You there! Where do you think you're going?"

Shoot! I'd been spotted. And by Dean, of all people. Now what? I turned and looked as innocent as I could. "What's the problem?" I asked. "I'm just going for a walk."

"With a backpack? Let's have a look. What's in there?"

Oh no. Even though I had the satellite phone

and my cell hidden under the false bottom, he would find the food I had packed for Ryan. I had to think fast.

"Just some of my stuff," I said, "and a bit of food."

He yanked my backpack open and peered into it, pulling out the food parcel that I'd wrapped up in paper napkins, holding up the bananas. "A *bit* of food? What's all this for? You're taking food to those kids in the jungle!"

"No way, man. I get really hungry between meals. There's no law against taking extra fruit and stuff from the dining room."

"You were heading for the out-of-bounds area with a backpack full of food. Come with me and explain it to Damien."

He was pulling out his two-way handset when I heard another voice—Sophie. My heart sank. What if she said something about how different I was? I'd told her that I had something personal planned. Stealing food for the runaways, she'd think. My mind was working overtime, trying to find plausible excuses.

Instead, to my complete surprise, Sophie linked her arm through mine, smiling up at the counselor while she spoke. "Ryan, you're such a dunce! This isn't the right place for our picnic. I meant over there, under the trees near the vegetable garden! Come on, can't you see that you're almost out of bounds here? Come this way." With that, she rolled her eyes at Dean, shaking her head as if to say, "Isn't he hopeless?" and started dragging me away in the opposite direction. Dean watched us go.

2:35 pm

As soon as we were a good distance away, Sophie stopped smiling, her face suddenly serious. She pulled me down onto the grass under the tree and kneeling opposite me, looked around to make sure that no one was watching or listening to us before she spoke. "OK, Ryan Ormond. What is going on? I just saved you from a whole lot of trouble. I think you owe me an explanation."

"You're right. I do. But I can't tell you. Please trust me!"

"Tell me right now, or else I'm going to march straight down there and report you to Damien myself." She started climbing to her feet.

"Please, Sophie, don't do that!"

She turned back to me, pointing a banana at me. "Explanation, please. Or I'm going."

She had me. I had to take a risk. If she'd taken a liking to my brother, I hoped I could trust her.

"OK," I said, "sit down. And stop waving that banana at me."

Sophie sat down, fixing me with her blue gaze. "Now," she demanded.

"You've noticed that I'm different—that I've changed?"

"A lot," she said. "You don't remember anything. You say crazy things. You seem totally—*dumb!* You even *look* different!"

"The truth is," I said, wondering how she would take this, "that I *am* different. Really different. I'm so different that I'm not actually Ryan."

Sophie Bellamy looked dumbfounded. She stared at me. "Huh? Have you gone completely nuts?"

"No. I'm not Ryan. I'm his twin brother, Cal."

Sophie's stare remained fixed for a few seconds then she blinked. "You're Cal Ormond? Not Ryan?"

"That's right."

"You're Cal? The twin brother?"

I nodded.

"The fugitive? Who had the whole country chasing him—and that girl—"

"Winter," I said. "Winter Frey."

"That's right. And your friend, Bugsy or—"

"Boges," I corrected.

"Boges," she repeated. "You guys were all over the news back then. He told me about his brother Cal. But—but where's Ryan?"

106

"He's hiding up in the jungle, halfway up the mountain."

"You were taking him food?"

"That's right. He injured his ankle and—well, it's a long story. So I'm taking his place for a while."

Sophie Bellamy stared out to the ocean, a slight frown on her forehead, her fair hair shining in the late afternoon sunshine, before turning her puzzled gaze on me. "You came here to check on Ryan?"

It was part of the truth and so I grabbed it. "That's right. I was worried about him."

I saw the relief in her face as she got a grasp on the situation.

She indicated the mountain with her eyes. "OK! What are we waiting for? Let's go visit him!"

I waited as Sophie slipped behind the large tree under whose shade we were sheltering, and when she was safely hidden, I took a quick look around and I gradually eased myself back into the undergrowth, melting into the thick jungle.

As we made our way up the rough path, Sophie told me about her own concerns. "Ryan and I have been talking. We both feel like there's something weird going down. Some of the kids adore Damien and would do anything for him. It all seems sunny on the surface, but what if it's not all water sports and campfire songs?"

"It seems more like a boot camp, don't you think?" I asked as we approached closer to where I'd left Ryan hiding.

"It sure feels like it sometimes," she said. "My father—" her voice faltered before she continued, "my father works in security and so I know a bit about that stuff . . . and I don't like the way the Paradise People Resort is run. It's more like an army barracks. All this roll call business and not being allowed to talk about certain things."

We paused, catching our breath. "What things?" I asked, curious.

"Well, we're not allowed to ask questions about the runaways. And both Ryan and I noticed other kids just disappearing. Not going home like most of them do, on the supply ship."

"What do you mean?" I asked.

"Most kids only stay a few weeks. Then they leave on the boat. But I've seen kids who were supposed to have gone home still here. It looks like they've gone home—they don't sleep in the dormitories anymore, their lockers are empty. But I've seen them—a few of them."

"Do you think the runaways and the disappearing kids are the same people?" I asked.

"There's no way of knowing because nobody really talks about it. I'd like to leave, but I've made friends here. I can't just run away and leave them. Not if something bad is happening. The disappeared kids must have gone somewhere." Sophie's blue eyes and freckled face were full of concern.

I whistled to Ryan to let him know that I was close to his hide-out and saw the curtain of vines and leaves move as he poked his head out. Sophie and I hurried over to him and he grinned widely to see us.

"Hey, Sophie! Cal!"

"How's that ankle, bro?" I asked, lifting away some vines and pushing through to Ryan's lair.

"Getting better . . . am I glad to see you! And you," he said to Sophie. "I guess Cal's explained our double act?"

"I was really confused until he did. I thought you'd gone totally crazy."

We crawled further into Ryan's cave and I pulled the food out of my backpack.

"I nearly didn't make it," I explained, telling him about the counselor who'd challenged me. "But Sophie saved the day." Then Sophie and Ryan shared their concerns about the disappearing kids and the runaways, whoever they were.

"What's really going on here?" asked Sophie.

"I'm hoping Cal can find out more about it. Damien asked me to join The Edge group. They do separate activities from the rest of the Paradise People," Ryan explained.

"I asked the matron of our dormitory, Mrs. Clayton, what happens to kids who don't fit in or who don't like this place," said Sophie, frowning. "She said they either go back with the supply ship if it's around or other arrangements are made for them to go home." She paused and her frown deepened. "But I don't believe that. Most of the counselors honestly believe Damien is only concerned for the safety of these so-called 'runaways,' considering the pythons and the stinging trees and other possible dangers on the island. I'm more worried about the kids who are supposed to have gone home and then I see them still here. I don't know where they live or what they do."

"Any ideas?" I asked.

"Not right now," she said. "But soon, I hope."

11:02 pm

Later that evening, I snuck out of the dormitory to call BB and got lucky with my phone reception. "I've seen Sophie and she's totally fine," I said. I could hear BB's sigh of relief down the phone line. "But listen, I want to stay longer," and I explained my idea of swapping with Ryan to find out more about the Paradise People.

"As long as you're confident you can handle the situation," BB said, "we'll let it play out for now. Just keep us posted and we'll wait to arrange your pickup. Over and out."

DAY 19

72 days to go . . .

Paradise People Resort

11:04 am

"Ryan Ormond, please report to Damien's office immediately." The announcement jolted me out of my thoughts as my name was blared over the loudspeaker. Did this mean trouble? I thought I'd blended in over the last day or so. Maybe not.

I hurried over to the main building and sat on a bench outside where a sign read: *Please wait here to see the team leader.* I waited for ten minutes, wondering what this was all about. Had Dean said something about finding "Ryan" out of bounds the other day?

I was getting more and more anxious when suddenly Damien himself appeared at the doorway, his powerful body almost filling the space. "Follow me, please, Ryan," he said, his face giving nothing away. I did so, taking in the steel staircase leading up to a second floor, with a number of doors leading off a corridor. At the end, we came to Damien's office.

"In here, please," he said, opening the door. I walked into a square room, two sides of which were thick glass overlooking the resort main square and many of the buildings, with a view to the mountain beyond. A long dark wood desk ran parallel to the eastern window. Along the opposite wall, a bank of monitor screens flickered, sending back live feed from the closed-circuit television cameras situated around the resort compound. A couple of the images were moving. Did Damien have roving hand-held cameras? Next to the screen on the wall, a number of keys hung on hooks.

As Damien ushered me to a chair, I tried to take a closer look. I could just make out some of the labels—"main gate," "D-1," "D-2," "D-11," "submersible." None particularly stood out, but could one of them be what Brittany Philips was scared of?

I took a seat in front of the desk. Damien could keep the resort under surveillance from this point, as well as watching a lot of the action of the Paradise People on the courts and grassy area at the beach. Two laptop computers on his desk rolled their screen savers.

He stood for a moment, his back to me, watching

a fast-moving basketball game down below, then turned to me and leaned forward on his desk. With an uncannily broad smile, he said, "Are you ready to give me an answer, Ryan? I'd hate for you to miss your chance. What do you say?"

Thank goodness Ryan had briefed me on this, I thought. I forced myself to return his big grin. "My answer is yes. I'd be honored to join The Edge."

Damien straightened up. "Good," he said. "Now that you're on board, I can tell you a little more about the squads. It's a program designed to help build strong, healthy bodies and minds. We combine adventure, healthy physical activities and survival challenges to nurture everyone's individual strengths. How does that sound to you?"

"Sounds pretty good," I said enthusiastically. I was warming up to my role now.

"When young people come here, they're often lost and lonely. We help them to reach their full potential with a great reward system—so they can strive to become the best they can be." He paused. "There is some pretty advanced training offered to the very best of them. But I'm getting ahead of myself. The next group after The Edge is extremely exclusive."

So there was another level, I thought to myself, even within the special program. Damien was smiling widely again. "There is however, the need for discretion. Your agreement to joining The Edge means you must not talk about it or about any of the extra activities that we offer. Not everyone who comes here is suitable for the program, and we can't provide it for everyone. It would be hurtful for other kids to find out and feel excluded, wouldn't it?"

"Sure, I understand," I said.

"So, not a word. When we're ready for you, one of the trainers will fly a small flag underneath the Paradise People Resort standard."

That must have been the darker pennant I'd noticed flying beneath the resort flag on my earlier reconnaissance.

Damien's phone rang and he hastily grabbed it, turning away from me. There was a few moments' silence as he listened to the caller, then in an urgent voice he said, "He can't have gone far. Deal with it!" He turned to me, flashing his smile again. "A lost dog," he explained.

I knew it was a lie. Damien was talking about someone who had gotten away. Someone who couldn't have gone far. Far from where? I still couldn't put my finger on what was wrong with this place. I didn't let any of my misgivings show as I put out my hand to shake his. "When do we start?" I said.

"Now is as good a time as any," he said. He pressed a button on a keyboard and within moments, a powerfully built man in army fatigues, his head shaven and with a jet earring flashing from his left ear, appeared at the doorway. "This is Hamish, Ryan. He'll take you to the others and put you through your paces. See what your strengths are so we can put you into the best program for your skill level."

He nodded to both of us to show that we were dismissed and I followed Hamish down the steel stairs, but this time we exited the building on the other side and into a large covered area that was easily as big as six basketball courts. Groups of kids were working through a gymnastics routine, others were wrestling, and a small group in white outfits were practicing martial arts with an instructor. This could be fun, I thought. Hamish turned to me and said, "Let's see what you can do. Start with push-ups."

I managed thirty-six.

"Not bad for a newbie," said Hamish, "I'll have you doing a hundred before long."

DAY 23

68 days to go . . .

Shadow Island Beach

8:52 pm

Over the next few days, I started training with eight other guys about my age. We also had a lot of fun kicking balls around and I was stoked to start learning abseiling with them.

At night, everyone would gather around a campfire on the beach, watching the moon rise out of the sea and singing at the tops of our voices while Damien joined in.

One night Sophie plopped down in the sand next to me, blowing on a sausage to cool it down, reaching out for the barbecue sauce that was being passed around the circle.

"I heard something interesting today. There's a rumor going around," she whispered to me as everybody laughed at one of Damien's jokes, "that there's someone on a rocky outcrop just south of the beach."

"What? Who?" I asked. But Sophie shook her head. "Nobody knows. It's just a rumor. It's probably not even true."

I looked across at Damien who was conducting some crazy song, using a piece of driftwood as a baton. "But it just might be," I whispered back.

11:13 pm

Later that night, I sneaked away to take food saved from our campfire feast to Ryan. As Ryan demolished a few cold sausages, we discussed the odd phone conversation I'd heard in Damien's office. "At least it wasn't me he was talking about," said Ryan.

"Maybe it was one of the runaways?" I suggested. "And Sophie told me a rumor she'd heard about somebody being kept prisoner on a rocky outcrop just past the island."

Ryan nodded. "I'd heard that too, but I just thought it was kids messing around—a campfire ghost story. But now I'm not so sure."

DAY 26

65 days to go . . .

Paradise People Resort

10:30 am

In the following days, our little gang went on six-mile runs, getting to see some of the amazing beauty of the island. With Hamish showing us where it was safe to go, we ran through lush jungle, along cliff tops with breathtaking views, and past a spectacular waterfall, where we often finished by jumping into the sparkling water and splashing each other. The uphill jogs carrying heavy packs to build up our endurance were less fun though.

In our stinger suits, we practiced our distance swimming and had a chance to enjoy the ocean too. As I swam past the rocky outcrop, I spotted a large square cement block behind the boulders and rocks of the small island. Could there be someone trapped out here? It seemed just too unbelievable.

Back in the covered court area behind the main building, we trained with weights, barbells and dumbbells. Hamish offered prizes and turned it into a competition. I did pretty well, but the super-strong guy in our group, Alex, seemed to be the best at winning extra desserts at dinner.

It was when we started practicing taking people by surprise from behind that I started to worry a bit. Why were we being trained in *this* sort of thing?

Then this morning at training there were only six of us. Puzzled, I asked Hamish. "Where are the other two guys?"

He fixed me with a steely gaze. "That's not something for us to worry about. Try sixty push-ups. Now."

As I puffed and grunted and sweated, straining over the last five, questions kept circling in my mind. Why were we training like this? Where had the missing two guys gone? Every day, Shadow Island and its popular and powerful leader raised more questions. From the basketball court I heard cheering and clapping as someone scored a basket. Other kids seemed to be happy, just having fun. Why was I so troubled about this place?

From now on, I needed to focus on finding the answers. At the back of my mind, I also had the nagging worry that almost four weeks had gone by since I'd received that mysterious text message. I was no nearer to figuring it out, but the days were still counting down.

1:41 pm

I saw Sophie Bellamy playing table tennis with another girl in the recreation room, her fair hair tied back into two braids, freckled face tense with concentration. I waited until she'd won the rally and sidled over to her. "Can we talk, in private?"

She nodded, and continued returning her opponent's serves with a killer spin until she'd won the game. She put her paddle down, shook hands with her opponent, threw a towel over her shoulder and dawdled over to join me. We stepped outside and I looked around to see where the nearest CCTV camera was positioned. I didn't want to be seen at all if I could help it.

"Let's go over to the cemetery," I said.

First we made as if we were preparing the kayaks to go out, scooping the water out of them, brushing sand off the hulls, then when we were certain no one was watching, we crawled past the bushes into the old graveyard.

"This place is creepy," Sophie said, looking around at the leaning tombstones and the almost-obliterated names and dates on them.

"They're OK," I said, "they're not going to say anything to Damien about us being out of bounds." I grinned.

"Where have you been?" Sophie demanded. "I've hardly seen you the last few days."

"I was invited to join The Edge," I said quietly. "I'm not supposed to say anything about it to anyone. I've been doing adventuring and training hard."

"Me too. Damien asked me a few days ago. I joined the girls' squad and got the same instructions about keeping it quiet. More secrecy."

I told her about the weird conversation I'd heard in Damien's office. Sophie was very skeptical. "Lost dog! There are no dogs here. He was talking about a person for sure. Let's see if Ryan has had any more ideas about it."

4:42 pm

As we crept out in the late afternoon to take food up to Ryan, I paused. "Sophie," I said. "I think you should leave."

"With you and Ryan still here? And all the other kids? No way!"

"OK, OK," I said. I knew exactly what she meant. I decided to make a call to BB later that night to brief him on our suspicions. But what we really needed was proof that something was up. "Sophie, I'm definitely going to stay here until we get some answers. So that way, you can go home, knowing that Ryan and I can deal with whatever is happening here."

I saw the look on her face. It said, *You're joking, right?* She rolled her eyes. "If Ryan's staying, and you are staying, so am I. Ryan is my friend!"

For the time being, I let the matter drop. I thought of her father and how he would worry if he knew about our concerns.

The three of us settled into Ryan's hide-out to discuss what to do.

"What do *you* think's going on here?" I asked my brother. "You've been here longer than me."

Ryan thought for a moment. "I get the feeling that there's some sort of *selection* process going on. Damien picks out certain kids who are really good at sports."

"What are they being selected *for?*" asked Sophie.

I was just about to ask another question when a sound made the three of us freeze. Someone or something was moving stealthily through the jungle near us. We shrank further back into our overhanging shelter, trying to be as invisible as possible.

I peered through a gap in the hanging vines. Two boys and a girl, all wearing bright-red-and-blue shirts, were creeping along the pathway. Ryan leaned closer, whispering in my ear. "I haven't seen these guys for weeks. What are they doing here?"

I waited until the small group had vanished from sight. "I'm going after them," I hissed.

"Me too," said Sophie.

"No, only me. Two people will make too much noise."

Lifting the veil of vines and creepers, I crept out from our hiding place, my eyes fixed on the spot where I'd last seen the trio. Moving as quickly as I dared, I went after them.

Ahead of me, I could see movement and the occasional flash of red-and-blue as I followed them further up the mountain. We were now high above the resort compound. Keeping my eyes peeled for pythons and stinging trees, I followed them for almost ten minutes. Then the sound of quiet voices carried on the wind to me. They seem to have stopped for a conversation.

Very carefully, I moved closer. I couldn't hear what they were saying, but I could see them quite clearly now, standing under a dense group of rainforest trees. The girl took out something small and black from her pocket and pointed it ahead of her. I noticed a wound on her upper left arm, just under what looked like a new tattoo — three lines, like a "Z." In surprise I saw that the boys had similar wounds and tattoos on their arms.

Before I had any more time to consider what it might mean, I heard a whirring sound. I crept closer and closer, trying to see what they were doing. Then I jumped back. I'd almost walked into another Gympie Gympie tree! I ducked around to avoid it, and when I'd straightened up the sound had stopped. I came forward, pressing close to a large rainforest tree, hoping to overhear their conversation. Now there was only silence and the occasional piercing sound of a rainforest bird. I peered around the tree, keeping my body well-hidden.

The trio had vanished! There was no one there. I blinked a couple of times, scarcely able to believe my eyes. One minute they'd been there, huddled together talking—the next minute they'd simply disappeared. I stepped out from behind the tree, wary of a trap. Maybe they knew they were being followed and set me up for an ambush. I took a few more careful steps towards the spot where I'd last seen the group. There was nothing to show anyone had been standing there apart from a faint footprint in the damp soil.

Ryan's Hide-out

5:29 pm

I jogged back to Sophie and Ryan, pushing aside the curtain of vines and creepers and squatted down beside them. They listened intently as I described what had happened. "They just disappeared," I said finally.

"But that's not possible," said Ryan. "Three people can't just vanish like that."

"I'm telling you what I saw. I know it sounds impossible."

"Did you hear anything strange?" asked Sophie.

"I did," I nodded. "Why? Have you heard something too?"

"Once I was up here exploring and I heard this odd noise, like machinery or an engine of some kind. I was surprised because I was in the middle of nowhere up in the rainforest."

"That's it!" I cried excitedly. "That's the sound I heard, too. A kind of mechanical sound."

The three of us looked at each other.

"Right," said Ryan. "So, some kind of machine?"

"The weird thing was," I said, "that all three of them had identical cuts and tattoos on their left arms—" I held my thumb and forefinger about an inch and a half apart—"the cut was really neat, and the tattoo was shaped like a 'Z.'"

"How about we go back there and take a look around?" Sophie suggested after a pause. "Three pairs of eyes are better than one."

I could see Ryan's ankle was finally healing well as we walked along the path the disappearing trio had taken until we came to the spot where I'd last seen them. We searched around, trying to find something—anything—that would explain what had just happened. But all we found was more rainforest and a massive rock face, dripping with moisture and mosses.

"I'd like to climb that," said Ryan, "if I had my gear."

"Wait till your ankle is completely healed," Sophie suggested. "There's climbing gear in the sports storeroom."

Finally, we had to give up searching. It was getting close to evening roll call and Sophie and I needed to be back at the resort.

"I'm going to move camp," said Ryan, "so I can be closer to that rock wall. I want to study it for finger holds."

We helped to move his gear further up the mountain and make another hide-out in another deep scoop in the rock, protected by overhanging foliage. "Careful of those Gympie Gympie trees up here," I said, pointing to two of the stinging trees that hung over the side of the new hide-out.

"That's my defense system," he said, grinning up at the overhanging leaves.

We quickly made our way back to the resort and could see kids waiting for evening roll call. Sophie and I split up in the cemetery, so that we could come in from different directions and avoid suspicion.

10:51 pm

That evening, I went in search of a safe spot to call BB. I wanted to text my mum as usual to stop her from worrying, and call Boges and Winter. I scouted around with my phone discreetly in my hand, looking for a place where the signal was strong and the likelihood of being spotted was minimal.

Overhead, thunder growled and the moon suddenly vanished. A tropical storm was about to dump all over me.

I found a spot just past the orange flags at the end of the beach. Here, the surf crashed and seethed around rocky black outcrops that jutted up out of the water. I was far enough away from the counselors not to be noticed if I squatted down behind a boulder. I called Boges.

"Great to hear from you, dude," said Boges.

"I'm here too," said Winter, chiming in.

"Hi there. How's it going back on the mainland?"

"Mmm. OK. What about you?"

"I can't talk for very long," I said, keeping an eye on the time so as not to miss BB. I told them how I'd found Sophie Bellamy, how Ryan had injured his ankle and I was now acting in his place. I told them of my suspicions about Damien Thoroughgood and the strange conversation in his office. "Kids are going missing," I said. "We actually saw it happen just a while ago." I relayed how the boys and girl in the red-and-blue shirts had vanished into thin air.

"Not possible, dude. They have to have gone somewhere."

I knew Boges was right, but it wasn't very helpful. I needed evidence.

"You told BB and SI-6 about Sophie, didn't you?" Winter asked.

"I spoke to him after I first arrived—he was happy to know Sophie is fine and safe. They asked me to have a look around too and that's what I'm doing now."

"Well, we haven't been sitting around doing nothing, either," said Boges. "Winter had a talk with Brittany Philips."

"How'd you manage that?" I asked.

"Having SI-6's resources on tap is quite cool, dude. I found an aunt of hers and it turns out

Brittany is staying with her. Winter managed to persuade Brittany to confide in her."

"Awesome! What did she say?"

"Not much, I'm afraid. She was pretty confused. She said she'd been fired because she'd overheard something," Winter said. "She's a really nice girl, but it's like she's got some sort of amnesia, or she doesn't want to talk," Winter added. "She had this wounded look about her."

That reminded me of something. "Did she talk about a cut or a tattoo on the arm?"

"No," said Winter, "but now that I think about it, she kept rubbing her arm, as if the muscle was aching or something. I thought it was just nerves. Why do you ask?"

I told them about the cuts and tattoos that I'd noticed on the upper arms of the disappearing trio.

"That's creepy," said Boges. "They sound deliberate—and surgical. What do you think the cut is for?"

"Not sure," I said. "It could be some sort of initiation. What about the key she mentioned?"

"I asked her about it, but she just clammed up. Wouldn't talk about it, no matter how much I tried to tell her we were on her side," Winter said, her concern evident in her voice.

"She's scared," I said.

"That's pretty clear. But scared of what? We need . . . before . . . you say so."

"Boges? Winter? You're breaking up."

Overhead, there was a loud clap of thunder and the storm clouds burst, heavy rain drumming on the ground.

"Boges?"

Nothing. The line was dead. I tried calling him again, and Winter's phone too, but nothing worked.

I looked at the time. This was my window to talk to BB. A huge crack of thunder right overhead made me nearly jump out of my skin. At the same time, a violent earthquake unbalanced me, and I fell, whacking my head against a low branch.

I tried to find some cover from the rain, running doubled-over towards the cemetery, where I found a little shelter beside a slanting headstone. But when I tried to call BB, there was nothing, not even static.

Defeated and dripping wet, I scurried back to the resort, hoping I wouldn't meet any staff on the way.

DAY 27

64 days to go . . .

Paradise People Resort

1:09 am

When everyone was asleep in the boys' dormitory, and the storm was well and truly over, I climbed out of bed and silently pulled the satellite phone out of my backpack. Even though it wasn't the right time, I felt I had to try again. Creeping to the door, I stepped out into the warm tropical night. The air was humid and oppressive and in the distance I could still hear thunder.

Keeping out of reach of the CCTV cameras, with the phone tucked safely inside my jacket, I quickly scaled the tall fence, dropping to the other side. I scuttled across to the shelter of the palm trees near the upturned kayaks.

I switched the phone on and dialed the number BB had organized. I was glad of the noise of the crashing surf nearby because there was loud static on the channel. Turned out that was all I could get—static.

I felt bad that I'd failed to talk to BB again. It'd be good to tell him how the next stage of my mission was going. I would have to make another attempt tomorrow night.

I crept back inside the dormitory, slipping past a couple of counselors who were huddled together having a late-night chat. I lay awake for a long time, trying to make sense of those identical wounds on the arms of the kids who'd disappeared, who'd somehow melted into the tropical jungle.

10:31 am

The next morning after breakfast, I searched around for Sophie with no luck. As I was looking for her, I'd noticed the small flag running up the flagpole—my call to training.

We trained and played particularly hard and I was red-faced and sweating, but satisfied with being on the winning team, by the time we finished. I was walking off the playing field when I heard someone approaching.

"You're doing very well, Ryan," said Ivan, the coach, catching up to me. "You're a natural. Have you done a lot of training before?"

"Kind of," I said, trying not to smile,

remembering how fit I'd become chasing the Ormond Riddle and Jewel halfway around the world.

"How do you feel about going up to the next level? Some of the activities can be more dangerous and we focus more on individual games. Like abseiling, adventure racing and martial arts katas."

I was being invited to join the elite of the elite. I could feel the smile getting away from me. I brought it under control. "I think I can handle it," I said. "I always like a challenge."

"Good. I'll settle it with Damien and then you and I can talk."

1:58 pm

After lunch, I went looking for Sophie. I searched everywhere. I went over to the girls' dormitory and knocked on the door. It was opened by a friendly-looking woman whose name I knew from Sophie.

"Excuse me, Mrs. Clayton," I asked, "I'm looking for Sophie Bellamy. Do you know where she might be?"

Mrs. Clayton frowned. "I'm afraid she's left," she said. "I think there was a problem at home. It's a real pity. She's a lovely girl, extremely smart. She was nice to have around."

I stood there in stunned surprise. Sophie was gone? It was hard to believe. In fact, it was impossible to believe, I started to realize. Something else must have happened.

Mrs. Clayton looked very sincere and I doubted she was lying to me. She was just passing on what she'd been told—probably by Damien.

"I'm sure she would have said goodbye to you, if it hadn't been an emergency," Mrs. Clayton said.

I walked away from the girls' dormitory, my thoughts whirling as I tried to find answers. Sophie had vanished—like the other kids who disappeared. I didn't believe for a minute that she'd had an emergency at home. I wasn't so sure about calling BB that evening. How could I tell him that I'd found Sophie, his precious daughter, and now she was missing?

Ryan's Hide-out

3:05 pm

While everyone's attention was focused on a game of soccer, I slipped away to see Ryan. I squatted down beside him, in his vine-covered lair, and pulled out the food supplies. He was very glad to see me, but his face soon dropped.

"Sophie's gone missing," I said. "We need to talk about what to do next. Mrs. Clayton, the woman who runs the girls' dormitory, told me some garbage about an emergency at home. She seemed to believe that Sophie had left the island during the night because of it."

"But wouldn't BB have said something when you called last night?"

I shook my head. "I couldn't get through. But maybe it's just as well. If they think something's happened to Sophie, they might come charging over to the island and then we'll never find out what's going on here."

"But what if she's in danger?" Ryan asked, frowning.

"I don't think she is in danger. I think she's been singled out to join whatever it is at the next level. My coach, Ivan, asked me how I felt about going to the next level too. My guess is that the kids who've disappeared join those ones we saw—the ones with the wounds and the tattoos on their arms."

"You think we should wait?" Ryan asked.

"Just a little. Let me figure out if there's anything else we can do. If not, I'll have to contact BB."

DAY 28

63 days to go . . .

Shadow Island Jungle

4:53 pm

The next day, I gave myself a headache trying to come up with a plan for finding Sophie, but it seemed like there was no other choice but to call for backup.

I jogged through the hot jungle on the now familiar path to Ryan's hide-out. Suddenly I heard a noise on the track behind me. I ducked behind some trees, crouching down just in time to hide from the girl in the red-and-blue shirt I'd seen disappear before. She sped past, oblivious to me. Silently, I got to my feet. I was *not* going to lose her this time.

It was easy to keep her in sight, following the flashes of her colorful shirt as she ran through the jungle. I recognized the path she was taking as the very same one I'd followed the trio along two days ago. A couple of times I saw her stop, turn around and stand still listening. Had she heard my footsteps behind her? I ducked down, crouching, until I saw her slowly turn around again and continue on her way. Soon she had arrived at the spot near the rock face that Ryan wanted to climb. Again, I saw her take something out of her pocket and again I heard the whirring noises.

I blinked in disbelief as the rock face moved!

Before my astounded eyes, the rock wall trembled and lifted up to reveal an opening, like a small garage door, through which the girl swiftly disappeared. I snapped out of my shock and ran after her, just managing to slip through the fast-narrowing gap as the grinding rock door closed behind me.

Mountain Bunker

5:14 pm

I took a few steps and stood in wonder. Above me, water glistened on a rocky ceiling. I was in a huge cavern. In front of me were descending steps carved into the mountain, and I caught a glimpse of the girl jumping the last few steps and running across the wide space beneath me. I realized this must be an underground military bunker. BB mentioned the island had been used during the Pacific War.

There, lit up by lights from powerful humming generators, a small squad of astonishingly precise teenagers were moving through their steps, each in perfect unison with their neighbors, so that they looked like a flash mob. I stood, breathless with admiration and surprise, watching them.

Carved in the rock wall behind them was a huge "Z." As they all turned sideways, I saw the small, straight wound on the upper left arm of each one. So, *this* was where the disappeared kids ended up, deep in the heart of the mountain. I searched their faces, but Sophie was not among them. *Where was she?*

As I watched, I spotted the coach, Ivan, who dismissed the group. They fell out of their precise formations, dissolving into a bunch of kids moving in different directions, picking up towels and packs and heading for underground corridors, where I could no longer see them, talking and laughing together. Soon all was quiet. I turned back to the rock wall entrance, but I had no idea how to get out. Maybe this was a one-way door—opening only from the outside, not from inside.

Suddenly, the lights went out and I was left in total darkness.

It took a little while for my eyes to adjust, but

there was some dim light from the corridors that gave out onto the wide arena space. I dug out my phone, and by its small beam, I cautiously made my way down the steps and onto the flat area, which I now realized was a natural cave of vast proportions. The sound of footsteps caused me to jump behind a craggy outcrop. I crouched down, listening.

"Chloe said she thought she heard someone up there," said a man's voice.

I peered around from my hiding place and saw someone I didn't recognize talking to Ivan.

"Someone could have come in behind her," he added. I froze as the lights suddenly came on. I shrank back as far as I could into the shadows. The footsteps came a little closer and then stopped. I held my breath. *Please don't come over here.*

"Maybe she's just imagining things," he said. "There's nobody here."

"OK, well, make sure Chloe understands that she has to be on her guard," Ivan said. "You know how important it is that only the Zenith team know of this place."

Zenith team! That must be what the tattoo stood for. I waited, barely daring to breathe, hoping like crazy that he'd say more.

"Especially now that everything's moving so

fast," Ivan continued, "they've only got a couple more months to go."

I heard them heading back towards the corridors, leaving me to exhale in relief, but feeling frustrated. What did Ivan mean? What were these kids doing in a couple of months' time?

As their footsteps faded, I was left with a bunch of questions and no answers.

I waited a while longer, wondering how on earth I was going to get out of the place. I couldn't go back the way I'd entered. If I wanted to get out of there, I would have to risk going down one of the corridors. I had no way of knowing if I'd be able to hide from people once in there and there'd be no bluffing my way out this time.

Missing evening roll call was going to be the least of my problems.

With my body tense with anxiety, on red alert, I made my way to the first of the corridors. Echoing further down, I could hear voices and the sound of crockery and cutlery. The Zenith team were at dinner. Maybe, just maybe, that would keep them out of my way while I tried to find an escape route. I sidled along the corridor, cut out of the mountainous rock, and sure enough, as I came closer to a lit doorway, the sounds of people dining became louder. I jumped across the light thrown into the corridor, hoping that nobody would look up and see me. I waited, tense, on the other side. But there was no outcry, no sound of rushing feet.

I kept going further and further down the sloping corridor, passing other doors as I went. A sudden rush of cooler air and the smell of salt hit me as I turned the corner. In front of me, the corridor widened out into another cavern, like a natural boat shed carved out of rock, leading out to a wide passage to the sea beyond.

The black water before me swirled around an amazing craft—sleek, streamlined and dolphin-shaped. Damien's submersible! With a windowed cabin at the front where the dolphin's "nose" would be, the slim silvery craft rose and fell on the slight swell. It was moored against a stone shelf of the cave which formed a natural wharf. But I didn't have time to admire the gleaming craft any further. I needed to get out of there— fast. I could hear voices moving down the corridor behind me.

I scrambled over the rocks on my right towards the low, wide archway that formed the entrance of the cave. I climbed awkwardly around until I had reached the opening to the sea.

I peered out, trying to get my bearings. Around a mile away, I could see the resort, further down the coastline. But to get back there, I'd have to make my way over the sharp and slippery rocks.

A sound behind me caused me to hide behind a couple of boulders. Dean stepped into view, staggering under the weight of some cartons. I watched through a crack in the rocks and saw him loading a small outboard motorboat that I hadn't noticed before, bobbing alongside the submersible. *Where was he going?*

For a minute, I thought he might have been making an escape from Shadow Island. But as I watched his careful movements while he loaded cartons into the motorboat, started the outboard and cast off, it was clear he wasn't in a hurry. It didn't take me long to figure out where he *was* headed—it had to be the rocky outcrop, the very small island that lay just off Shadow Island!

I waited until Dean was out of sight, then I set off, using both hands to steady myself. Sometimes I could only crawl on all fours, getting completely soaked in the process. All the time, my mind was churning crazily. Was there a prisoner on the rocky outcrop? I was determined to find out. Now that I'd seen where the small outboard craft was kept, I could use it to cross the water myself and have a look around. There was no other choice now, I had to investigate.

It was now even more imperative to contact BB at the appointed time. I continued my slow and rocky climb back to the resort.

Shadow Island Beach

8:54 pm

I'd made my excuses about missing roll call, but had been told I'd need to explain myself to Damien in the morning. I kept a low profile after dinner and wandered innocently to the water's edge while the counselors on duty were chatting together.

Fast as I could move while doubled over, I scrambled past the end of the beach, keeping out of the reach of the biggest waves. I climbed over the rocks, but I could barely see, scraping my knees and hands painfully in my determination to get back to the secret cave. It seemed to take forever, and once a wave broke right over me and I had to cling on to jagged rocks in order not to be swept away. I was really scared that a big wave might carry a stinger with it and that would be the end of me.

Eventually, I got to the looming blackness which I knew was the mouth of the large cavern. I clambered up onto the rocky ledge, slowly making my way as my eyes adjusted. I wound my way past the dolphin-shaped vessel to where the motorboat bobbed. I jumped in and steadied it as it rocked from side to side. The black water and the rocky cavernous ceiling reminded me of the huge underground lake over which Repro and I had rowed when I helped him shift his camp. I smiled to myself. Repro would have been in his element here.

I found the oars on the bottom of the boat and pushed them into the oarlocks. I had to row—I didn't dare use the engine so close to the underground tunnels.

I pushed away from the wharf towards the open ocean, taking my time to settle into a good rhythm.

As I rowed across the water, easily negotiating a mild swell, I felt a heaviness lift from me. I realized that here in the boat, was the first time since I'd been on Shadow Island that I'd actually felt *free*. There were no counselors to avoid, no CCTV cameras to keep away from, no roll calls—just me, the sea, the sky and the stars overhead. I could almost imagine Dad in the boat with me. I remember Dad once doing a story about a prisoner of conscience, saying, *"There's only one thing worse than having your life taken from you, and that's having your freedom taken away."*

Rocky Outcrop

9:47 pm

Finally I was approaching the rocky outcrop and I could see a sloping stony beach. I manipulated the boat in the shallower water until I could jump out safely. I used a wave surge to push the boat up high away from the tidemark. I heaved it once more to lodge it behind some rocks. I sure didn't want to be trapped here without a boat.

I clambered across the rocks to where I could see a building rising up from the flat, stony ground. As I came closer, I flashed my phone light around. In its cold beam, I could make out a low cement bunker, almost rectangular in shape, the size of an average one-story house. But this "house" had no windows, just narrow gun slits. The whole place reminded me of the old bunker system that Gabbi and I played in on Bare Island years ago. As I crunched around the perimeter of the square building, I came to one narrow, barred window, about ten feet from the ground. Now I was *certain* this was a prison.

The rumors on Shadow Island were that someone was locked up here in this horribly desolate place. Was that true?

Scooping up a handful of small stones, I threw them at the bars of the window. They rattled down to the ground. I was bending to gather another handful when the sound of a man's voice shocked me. It was coming from behind the bars. "Help me," he groaned. "Help me!"

"Who are you?" I called back.

There was a long silence. I repeated my question. Finally, after another long silence, the groaning voice spoke again, halting gaps between each word, "I—don't—know. Help me. Please."

"I will," I said. At that moment, I had no idea how I could help this prisoner, but I couldn't leave anyone in a place like this without trying. "What's your name?"

Again came the croaking voice, "I—don't—know!"

This time, I could hear the anguish and despair in his voice. He really didn't know.

Something made me turn around and I freaked out when I saw a strong light sweeping over the water as the sound of a boat penetrated the noise of wind and waves. Somebody else was heading this way! Desperate, I looked around me, but there was nowhere to run. There was nowhere to hide. The chugging noise of the boat came closer and closer and the beam of light continued to sweep the ocean. I flattened myself against the cold cement of the bunker, wondering if I could make it back to the rocks. As the craft approached, I could see it was the submersible, but riding high in the water, searching for the outboard motorboat—and me.

The light flashed over the rocky outcrop, sweeping the walls of the cement bunker. I dashed around the corner to avoid its probing beam. Then I ran to the next corner as the submersible searchlight flashed over the wall I had pressed against only seconds earlier. My heart was pounding in my ears. Any minute now they'd find me.

Amazingly, after covering the rocky outcrop with the powerful light, the submersible just continued on its way, heading north up the coast, searching the waters around Shadow Island. They hadn't seen me or the boat! I breathed a huge sigh of relief.

I calculated I had enough time to get back by the time they had circumnavigated the whole island and come back to the cavern mooring. As I ran back to the boat, I paused at the wall. "I'm sorry, I have to go or they'll catch me!" I shouted up. "I promise I'll come back." But there was silence from within. My heart sank to leave someone there, but I had to go or there would be no chance of escape for either of us.

I rowed back as fast as I could and breathed

another sigh of relief as the cavern came into view. With aching arms, I rowed over to the wharf, roping the craft until I got out, then freed it and watched it drift towards the opening to the ocean. Hopefully they'd think it had drifted off its mooring.

I kept moving, climbing over rocks, avoiding the deep crevices between them and the surging waves that frothed up through the narrow channels. Even though the surf here was reasonably low, eddies and jets of cold water sprayed all over me as the water slapped against the uneven shale and boulder-strewn edge of Shadow Island.

Finally, soaking wet, I made it to the sandy headland that ran out into the sea not far from the resort compound. Now all I had to do was get back inside safely.

Paradise People Resort

11:28 pm

Then I saw the time.

I couldn't believe it! I'd missed the window to contact BB. But there was no point in kicking myself. Maybe there was a chance that the channel was still open. I tried calling BB again, but my luck had run out for the day.

Back at the boys' dormitory, I saw my name on the bulletin board near the door. I was to report to Damien's office after breakfast and explain why I had missed evening roll call.

I was wondering what excuse I could possibly make when something whizzed past my head! Instinctively, I ducked. I looked up to see an arrow shuddering in the wood frame of the bulletin board. I craned around. All I could see and hear past the lit area was the darkness of the night and the occasional rustle of the palm trees.

I threw myself back down on the ground, scared and shocked. I waited. Nothing happened. Nothing moved. Cautiously, I climbed to my feet, pulling the arrow out of the wood when I noticed something—a wad of paper tied around its shaft. I took the arrow into the dormitory with me, pulled my sneakers off and climbed into my bed. I untied the folded paper, and hiding my phone light under my blanket, smoothed the piece of paper out. It was a very brief message—

Your friend Sophie is being held inside the mountain. She needs your help.

Where had this come from? Was it from one of the Zenith team?

I lay awake, trying to figure things out. If the message was from someone at the resort, why deliver it in such a dramatic fashion? It could have been tucked under my pillow or under my placemat in the dining room. Could this be the work of the mysterious runaways—whoever they were?

DAY 29

62 days to go . . .

9:03 am

The next morning, I was standing in front of Damien in his office as he looked at me sternly. "So, you got lost, did you?"

There hadn't been any reference to the events of the night before. Maybe I'd gotten away with it, and someone had retrieved the boat, and as I had hoped, assumed it had somehow come loose on its own. But right now, I had to find a convincing story to cover myself.

I told him part of the truth about what had happened yesterday evening as I made my way around the coast. "I didn't realize that I'd wandered off," I said. "I was exploring the rocky area over by the beach. I went further than I'd planned. And then it started getting dark. I tried going inland a bit, but then I think I must have gone around in a circle, the way you do when you're lost."

"It's just that we worry, Ryan. I'm sure you

understand. Your safety is our number one priority," said Damien. "As long as it doesn't happen again. I hope I haven't misjudged you. I like your initiative, but it's also very important to obey the rules. Paradise People—*real* Paradise People," he said, his tall figure suddenly towering over me, "are people who know how to follow rules—who know how to obey orders without question."

As Damien looked away, I strained to look at a bunch of keys on his desk, but I couldn't read the tag attached to them. For some reason, they looked like the ones Dad used to throw down on the kitchen counter when he came home. I thought of our times together at Treachery Bay. Those days seemed to belong to someone else's life now. I pulled myself away from the sadness by wondering if those keys were for Damien's submersible.

I nodded when Damien turned to me again, doing my best to look meek and apologetic. "Did you ever find that lost dog, Damien?" I asked innocently.

For a second, Damien looked completely bewildered. He's forgotten that lie, I thought. But he rallied quickly. "Oh, the *dog*," he said. "Oh yes, we did." His smile was forced. "Off you go then, Ryan."

"Thank you, sir," I said, and turning to go, I noted the other keys hanging temptingly on the key rack.

As I left Damien's office, I tried to look suitably contrite. Right now I was desperate to make contact with whoever had sent me the message about Sophie. And then I would help the prisoner on the rocky outcrop.

Ryan's Hide-out

10:12 am

An hour later, I found a quiet moment to head back into the rainforest, along the sketchy pathway. At Ryan's hide-out, I called Boges as Ryan hungrily ate the breakfast I'd brought him.

"Sophie is in trouble," I said when he answered. I told him what I'd discovered behind the rock face, about my visit to the bunker on the desolate island off the coast of Shadow Island. "Someone is locked up there," I said, "and he's asked for help."

"Who is it?"

"He says he doesn't know."

"Not good, dude. Have you spoken to BB? Do you want me to call him? This is getting seriously out of hand."

"I've had communication problems and I was going to try again tonight." I thought a moment.

"The problem is, Boges, that it's not only Sophie who might be in trouble. Or even that prisoner. I'm worried in case there's a much bigger problem here than any of us thought. If SI-6 launch a full-scale raid, I get the feeling that Damien could be quite ruthless."

"And do what?"

"Something to hide the evidence. Maybe even hurt people." I pulled out the message from the arrow, showing it to Ryan. "This was fired just over my head last night," I said.

Ryan read the note. "We've got to get her back, Cal," he said.

"Dude, what's happening?" Boges asked.

I told Boges about the message delivered by arrow. "Ryan and I are going to see if we can make contact with whoever sent it."

"But, Cal," said Boges, "they might be some lost tribe of headhunters living in the jungle! You don't know what's on that island!"

"Boges, I don't think headhunters would write a message, in English, about helping a friend of mine."

"OK, OK, I guess I'm exaggerating a *little*," said Boges. "But these people have bows and arrows. You'd better be careful."

"I will. We will."

"I have some news too," Boges said. "Winter

has spent some more time with Brittany Philips. She said she can't remember anything more about a key except for one word—Mordred. She refused to have anything to do with it, but she can't remember why. And yes, I looked up what Mordred might refer to. The only thing I can find is that Mordred was a character in the legend of King Arthur. He was an enemy of the king, *not* a good guy. Not sure that's much use to you, dude."

I was about to ask more when Ryan kicked me hard.

"Hey!" But then I saw the expression on his face. *Fear.*

He was looking straight past me, through the gaps in the creepers that covered the front of his hide-out. His voice was a low hiss. "Cal! There's someone out there!"

I abruptly hung up on Boges, shoving my phone under a pile of Ryan's clothing. Cautiously, I got to my knees and looked through the gaps.

And looked straight into the eyes of a boy, about my age, who stood just a few yards away with a drawn arrow pointed right at my head!

"Come out of there!" he ordered. "Both of you!"

For a moment, I was immobilized with fear. But surely this boy didn't mean me any harm, if he was the one who had sent the message about Sophie. Though the arrow begged to differ.

"We'll come out," I said, "if you point that thing in another direction."

Slowly the boy lowered the bow and arrow, and as he did, I saw a girl, similarly armed, standing just behind him. Their dirty clothes were threadbare and both of them were heavily tanned and barefoot, with long dark hair flowing over their shoulders. Slowly, Ryan and I crawled out of the hide-out, straightening up and standing in front of the two of them.

"Who *are* you?" I asked. "Did one of you fire that message last night?"

"Come with us," said the girl.

Ryan and I did as we were asked, following the girl, who led the way, while the tough-looking boy brought up the rear. We walked through rugged and overgrown jungle, our feet squishing in the mud which was becoming heavier the higher we went. As we walked, I realized that the pair might know a lot more about Shadow Island than I did. It was probably best to cooperate unless I sensed we were in real danger.

Runaways' Cave

11:09 am

At last we stopped at a particularly thick clump of overgrown rainforest trees, knitted together with vines and creepers to form a seemingly impenetrable green wall. I was startled to see the girl easily raise a dense, leafy bough to reveal a small, dark opening. She pointed to show I should crawl through. I hesitated a moment, but a prod from the boy's arrow decided for me.

I crouched down and crawled through the opening, looking up in surprise as I saw where I was. In front of me was another arching cavern, smaller than the large one hidden behind the secret entrance in the rock, furnished with blankets and cushions and lit from above by a hole in the ceiling which allowed slanting sunlight to fall on the cave floor. I stepped further in and waited while the others came through. Runaways or not, these two knew how to make a comfortable hide-out.

"How about you tell us who you are?" I asked. "And then we'll tell you more about who we are."

"You're Cal Ormond," said the boy, "and he's Ryan Ormond. Right?"

"So obviously you've been watching us for a while," I said.

There was a hint of a smile on the boy's stern, sunburned face. "Could be," he said. Then he put his hand out. "I'm Zak Katz."

"And I'm Ariel," said the girl, lowering her bow and arrow. "We've had you two under surveillance for a while. It's not every day someone lands by paraglider and then swaps places with another guy who looks exactly the same as him."

"You must be the runaways," I said.

"That's what *he* calls us."

"So you did send the message about Sophie?" I said.

"Yes," said Zak.

"She was running away, but they caught her," Ariel said. "She kept yelling out 'No way! It's not going to happen!' And then we saw her get taken into the mountain. We'd overheard some of your conversations about Sophie and about the situation here on Shadow Island."

"Sounds like we're all on the same side," Ryan said. "Maybe we should all shake hands and swap information. See what we can come up with together?"

I noticed a small smile start on Ariel's face, twinkling her eyes.

The atmosphere in the cave suddenly warmed, Zak and Ariel put down their weapons and pulled up boxes for us to sit on, while they brought out something to drink. "The drink carton was heavy, but we managed to steal it from the supply ship," Ariel grinned, passing them around. "We've gotten pretty good at raiding food. And there's always some kind of fruit ripening in the rainforest. We don't cook because the smoke would give away our location. And so far it hasn't gotten too cold."

"How long have you two been here?" I asked.

"Zak and I ran away from the resort nearly three months ago," Ariel explained. "He's my brother." She sighed. "At first, we loved the place. We weren't happy at home when our parents split. Dad went overseas and Mum had this new boyfriend who couldn't stand us. That's when we decided to go. We heard about this place and thought it sounded great. The Paradise People seemed really cool and for a while we were glad to be here. Especially when we were both picked from The Edge to join the Zenith team."

"So what went wrong?"

"The initiation—we didn't want to be involved in that," Zak said.

"You mean that wound on the arm?" I asked, sitting up straight.

Ariel nodded as Zak continued. "They explained it to us as a lesson in trust. Like how people in the olden days used to cut their arms and mix their blood to swear loyalty to each other? Something like that. I wasn't too keen on it so when Ariel refused, so did I. Man, did that get us into strife! They told us that nobody else had ever refused and that it meant that we weren't team players and weren't suitable to be in the program anymore. We're guessing that Sophie didn't want it either."

"So then what happened?" asked Ryan.

"They said they were going to send us back when the next supply ship came because we 'no longer upheld the high values of striving for excellence and loyalty to team members.'"

"So, if Sophie also rejected the idea of the initiation," I said, "we can assume she got the same kind of lecture and treatment?"

"It's our best theory so far," said Zak. "We were locked up and I reckon she is, too. Maybe they've decided to hold her inside the mountain to make sure she doesn't run away like we did."

"We were cool with not being in the The Edge anymore. We'd learned a lot about ourselves and decided we'd go home and explain things to Mum—try to get her to understand. Work it out with her instead of just running away again."

"And then?" I asked, riveted by their story.

"But then we discovered it wasn't going to be that simple," Ariel said. "We were in disgrace, kept apart from everyone, like we had a disease or something. Zak was held near Damien's office, and I was in one of the smaller storage rooms."

"The morning before the supply ship came in, I saw Brittany through the window, running like crazy towards the room where I was. She had two counselors and Damien after her. She burst through the door and came racing in—almost knocked me over. She pressed something into my hand just before they grabbed her. She said, "Help him! He knows what's going on! He says there are others, too!" and then they hauled her away."

"Who do you think she meant?" I asked, extremely anxious now. "What others?"

"We don't know. All I know," she said, "is that there was an announcement at roll call that Brittany had taken a stinger suit without permission and gone swimming near the outcrop where it's really dangerous. But that's not why she was fired. We think she got too close to the truth about what's going on. We've heard the rumors about someone being locked up out there."

"Actually, it's a fact," I said, and I told them about my night journey to the outcrop and the strange man who didn't know who he was.

Ryan's question interrupted my thoughts. "What did Brittany pass you?"

Ariel searched around in a small box on the floor of the cave. "This. I wish I knew what it meant," she added, passing it to me. It looked like a name tag of some sort, one that had been pulled off something.

I stared at it, staring at the triangle with the two lines inside it. "Can you make any sense of it?" I asked Ryan, handing it to him. He looked at it for a moment and then passed it back, shaking his head.

"Not really. It looks kind of mathematical. Could it be something to do with a key? Could it have come off a key ring?"

"Why a key?" Ariel asked.

"Brittany had nightmares after she got back from here," I said. "She spent some time at a center where a friend of mine has done some volunteer work. According to the woman who runs the place, Brittany would yell out in her sleep about some kind of key—she was really upset about it."

I pulled out my phone and took a picture of the mysterious triangle and emailed it to Winter. She'd made sense of strange symbols before. Maybe she could figure this out, too. "I'm sending it to a friend of mine," I explained to Ariel and Zak.

"She's really good with codes and languages," Ryan added.

"She's working on the mainland," I said, "doing what she can to help me over here."

The four of us sat in silence for a while, and I worried about Sophie and finding her.

"Cal, you've gotta call BB," Ryan suggested, his face serious. "I don't like the sound of what's happened to Sophie."

"Who's BB?" Ariel and Zak asked together.

"Sophie's father," I said. "He was worried about his daughter." There was no need to reveal everything—I stuck to my simplified version of events. "Everything seemed to be all right, but then she suddenly disappeared. And from what you've told us, we've got a reason to worry. I'm going to get inside the mountain and find Sophie," I said. "But I might need some help."

"I'll come with you," said Ryan.

"Better you go back to the resort," I said. "You need some good food, a warm bed and a hot shower."

I filled him in on how I'd been recruited for the Zenith team so that he could take over. "How's your fitness level?" I joked.

"It was pretty good until I did this," said my brother, pointing to his injured ankle. "If Hamish notices anything, I'll tell him I had a relapse. I'd better go."

We swapped clothes and gave each other a high-five. "Keep your eyes peeled for anything helpful," I said. "In case there is anything I need to know."

"How are you going to get in there?" Zak asked, when I'd rejoined them in the cave.

"I suppose I could wait until training tonight, now that I'm a member of the Zenith team. But I don't really want to wait that long and I might not be able to do a full search if I'm meant to be training," I said. I looked at Zak and Ariel and wondered if they would help me. "What do you guys think?" I said.

"We want to know what's going on here just as much as you do," said Ariel. "We're getting a bit sick of living like Robinson Crusoe."

"And this might come in handy too," Zak said, as he pulled out a piece of folder paper. "This is a map of the *real* Shadow Island."

"Wow," I said. "Cool. So, let's make a plan."

And that's exactly what we did.

WELCOME TO
SHADOW
ISLAND

the real

volcano

W-W

Outside Mountain Bunker

3:41 pm

I'd cleared out Ryan's hide-out, taking the clothes and rations back to Zak and Ariel's cave, and I'd made up my mind that I'd contact BB to organize a pickup as soon as possible. Maybe Sophie would be willing to leave the island now that her situation had become more precarious.

Now I was well-hidden behind rainforest plants not far from the rock face, waiting for an opportunity to get inside. The mosquitoes were becoming very annoying and I rubbed some lemon-scented herbs that Ariel had given me over my bare arms and face. I heard a noise and strained to hear what was happening. I could hear people jogging through the thick rainforest jungle. It must be a Zenith team. I shrank down, hoping I was invisible in the undergrowth.

The whirring sound started as the group approached and I saw that the trainer was holding a remote in his hand. I watched once more as the door in the mountainside opened. The team disappeared through it, followed by their trainer. As it started to close, I dashed forward, a small tree branch in my hands, and just made it, squeezing through with only seconds to spare. Quickly I jammed in the branch, leaving a narrow crack in the door, just big enough for someone to squeeze through. I hoped no one would notice.

Once inside, I froze, not daring to move until my eyes had adjusted to the dim light and I could be sure I hadn't been seen.

Just like before, the kids regrouped in the small arena beneath me. Staying low, I watched their breathtaking martial arts display. These guys were good—very good. They could have been part of an Olympic team. One girl threw a grappling hook attached to a long rope high up into the ceiling of the huge cavern where it caught and anchored. A few strong tugs to make sure it was securely lodged, and then she seemed to *run* up the wall like a superhero. I'd never seen anything like it. Finally, they finished their training session with some astonishing sparring, taking each other down in a blur of speed. Would joining the Zenith team make me able to climb and fight like this too?

The team had finished its workout and now were heading down the corridor. This was my chance.

As quietly as I could, I crept towards the corridor. The sound of people chattering filled the narrow space. Silently, I checked out the first door on my right. It opened easily and from the light in the corridor, I could see that it was a storeroom, with shelves piled high with food. I closed the door and sneaked along to the next one. This one too was filled, this time with sporting gear, bicycles, racquets, a couple of vaulting horses and gym gear. Now came the most dangerous part—getting past the dining room. I was about to close the door of the equipment room when I heard footsteps coming up behind me. Quick as a flash, I dived into the room and closed the door, leaving a tiny crack to look through. It was Damien, striding along purposefully. I feverishly hoped he wasn't looking for equipment.

He walked straight past and into the dining room. Phew! At least that will keep them occupied, I thought. The chattering din in the dining room quickly subsided as he began to speak in his commanding voice, "Ladies and gentlemen of the Zenith squad . . . "

I noticed to my dismay that he'd pushed the door right open when he went in. I groaned. It would now be even harder to get past without being seen. I didn't want to end up like Sophie, locked up and powerless. As Ryan, I already had a couple of black marks against my name. Being caught down here was bound to create a whole new set of problems for me.

There were two more doors further down the hallway, half-concealed in darkness. I had to check those rooms. That meant I had to get past the dining room. I started tiptoeing along the wall, listening to Damien's ringing voice as he praised and complimented his elite athletes. Walking steadily and without any sudden moves that might catch people's peripheral vision, I slowly walked past the wide-open door. From the corner of my eye I could see everyone was facing Damien. *Don't turn around, anyone, please,* I prayed. If I was spotted, I hoped that Ariel and Zak would activate their part of the plan.

Bit by bit, I edged across until finally I'd gotten past the doorway. I'd done it!

But a sudden silence from the dining room froze me in fear. I heard footsteps from the dining room, heading my way.

What could I do? Where could I go?

I was about to make a desperate dash for the end of the corridor and the exit out to the coast when to my surprise, the door to the dining room was suddenly shut.

I leaned against the wall and let out a huge breath of relief. The silence had not been about me after all. Whatever the reason, it gave me a break.

With no time to wait for my heartbeat and breathing to return to normal, I approached the remaining doors. The first one was locked.

041

I pressed my mouth close to the crack in the door. "Sophie?" I hissed. "Sophie, are you there?" Nothing. I tried again.

Behind me, I heard the dining room door being thrown open. I pressed myself flat against the first door, trying to take cover in the slight recess. But it wasn't going to hide me for long, and the voices and the footsteps were coming closer. Any moment now I'd be discovered. *Ariel and Zak! Where are you?*

A commotion further away came like an answer to my silent cry. The footsteps and voices abruptly turned, going back the other way down the corridor, away from me. The runaways had arrived, sneaking through the rocky doorway I'd propped open.

I knew I only had a few minutes. Ariel and Zak could divert the Zenith team for a while, but I couldn't rely on too much time.

I raced to the second door. "Sophie! Are you there?" I called, louder now. "It's me, Cal."

The answer was almost immediate. "Cal? Cal? Really? Is it you?"

"It's me!" I said.

"Please help me, I'm locked in here!" Sophie cried. "Can you open the door?"

I tried turning and twisting the door handle, but to no avail. It would not open.

Behind me, the cries and running footsteps were becoming louder.

"Sophie, I can't open the door. But I'm going to get you out of here, OK? And then off the island. But I have to go now." As I looked at the locked door, I saw a small sign next to it—*D-2*. I recalled some of the keys I'd seen hanging on Damien's key panel—D-1 and D-2. I knew what I had to do!

Shouts came towards me. "Lock her up!" I heard Damien yell and then Ariel shouting out, "Let me go! You have no right to do this! Get your hands off me!"

They'd captured Ariel! No! What sort of a retreat was this where people get *captured?* I couldn't wait any longer. "Sophie, don't give up. I'll be back as soon as I can. OK?"

"Please! It's awful being locked up like this!"

The fear and desperation in Sophie's voice jolted me. This was way out of line. Damien had every right to run the resort the way he wanted to, even with his silly rules and programs.

But not this.

Locking people up, depriving them of their freedom—this was outright *criminal* behavior. The situation was getting too much to handle. Tonight, I'd tell BB everything. I couldn't risk waiting any longer.

I darted down the narrow corridor heading for

the exit at the waterside. I felt like a rat running away while two friends were in trouble, but it was essential that I get away. Ryan, Zak and I were the only ones who could help them now.

I had to get into Damien's office and get the key to D-2, and get everyone to safety. My mission was getting bigger by the minute.

I wished Repro was there as I made my way back around the coast, slipping and sliding on the slimy rocks, dodging the waves that crashed over me. He would have had the door to D-2 open in a flash. And he would have helped me release the unknown prisoner trapped across the water.

Paradise People Resort

10:02 pm

I'd gotten back, drenched and shivering, racking my brain trying to think of a way to get to those keys in Damien's office. But I had to bide my time. Eventually all seemed quiet and the coast looked clear. I took a running jump at the resort gate and climbed over it, jumping down, and running towards my dormitory.

"Hey! Who's that?" The sudden voice shocked me. A nearby counselor had seen or heard something.

I ducked behind a bush near the clotheslines

area, pulling myself into a ball, trying to be part of the prickly shrub. I saw feet walk by as they checked out the area and watched the circular pool of light from a flashlight wavering over the ground. I held my breath. The flashlight moved past, heading for the fence, piercing the darkness of the night. It lit the palm trees further away near the end of the grassy area towards the beach. After a final pause, they moved on.

I crept to the window nearest the bed where both Ryan and I had slept. I could see my brother, snoring his head off. I threw a small stone in through the window which hit his shoulder. Ryan woke up with a shock, jumping up, about to yell out.

"Quiet!" I hissed.

He saw me at the window. "What's going on?" He didn't look too thrilled at what I had to say. "We've got to swap over."

"Again?" he whispered, padding over to the window. "Just when I was getting used to the good life. I *like* sleeping in a bed. I'm getting a bit tired of being your body double."

"C'mon, Ryan. I need to be here. I know where Sophie is, but I need to get into Damien's office—I've seen the key I need. And there's some bad news—Ariel's been captured too."

"When? What happened?"

Ryan got dressed. The rest of the sleepers snored on and we crept out of the dormitory and slid along the building until we were in a dark corner away from the CCTV cameras. I told Ryan about what had happened in the mountain and how I'd heard Ariel yelling. "I've tried radioing SI-6, but I haven't had any luck so far."

"I could do it," said my brother.

I shook my head. "No. I can do it. I'll try again from another position."

"I'll go find Zak and make sure he's OK," said Ryan.

"Thanks, bro. Good luck," I said giving him a farewell bearhug.

10:56 pm

I dozed fitfully for half an hour, and finally picked up my charged phone and crept outside. In a sheltered spot between two huge boulders some distance from the cemetery, I pulled out the satellite phone. I selected the secure channel. "Condor, Condor. Night Hawk calling Condor. Do you read me?"

The only reply was the sound of static. I tried again with the same result. I looked up at the looming mountain. For some reason, I simply wasn't getting through. I would have to try again higher up. Or maybe there was something wrong with the phone? I tried one more time and then gave up.

Knowing she would be surprised at this hour, I called Winter. "Hey, it's me," I whispered when I heard her sleepy, grumpy voice.

"Grrrr . . ." she growled. "Do you know what time it is?"

"Sorry. But I need you."

"You say the nicest things. So, what do you need?"

"Have you had a chance to look at that torn tag I emailed you? The one Brittany managed to give to Ariel?"

"The triangle with the two lines in it? I think there are a number of ways it can be read. It's the shape of the Greek letter delta, so it'd be something like delta double one or delta 11."

"That's brilliant," I said, alerted and excited, recalling the label on the key I'd seen hanging on Damien's key rack—D-11. "And I've just realized something," I added. "Sophie is being held in a room called D-2—the door next to hers is D-1."

"Delta 1 and Delta 2!" Winter said.

"Winter, you're a genius."

"Don't tell Boges. He thinks he's the only genius on our team."

"Promise I won't. But right now I've got a bigger question for you."

"Only if you tell me everything that has happened since we last talked."

I dutifully brought her up to date—about the prisoner on the outcrop, meeting Ariel and Zak, the unbelievable skills of the Zenith team and all my concerns about what was really going on under the happy veneer of the Paradise People Resort.

"Sophie and Ariel are locked up? And there's another prisoner, and maybe others too? Cal, this is out of control now, you have to tell SI-6 everything!" Winter said.

"I know you're right, but they don't know I'm here so we've still got that advantage. If it looks like I can't get them out, I'll call in the troops. I promise, OK?"

I could hear Winter muttering something about foolish bravado. But finally, I got to the question I wanted to ask her.

"So, the word Mordred—what does it mean to you? Boges told me he was an enemy of King Arthur, but I mean what images or what things come to mind when you think of it? Text me with any ideas. They might help."

"OK, I promise I'll get back to you on this one after I've done some research, and there's something else you should consider."

"What's that?" I asked.

"If there's Delta 1 and 2, and also Delta 11 . . ."

"Somewhere, there's probably Delta 3 all the way up to 10," I finished her thought.

"Exactly."

"With kids locked up in them," I said.

"Could be," Winter said.

"That's a horrible thought."

"I'll talk to Repro. He might have some ideas," Winter said.

"I've already got a plan," I said.

DAY 30

61 days to go . . .

3:00 pm

That day, I went to training as usual, waiting for my call up to the Zenith team, throwing myself into it while my mind was almost in meltdown. I rehearsed over and over how I was going to get inside Damien's office, grab the key to Delta 2, free Sophie and then contact BB so that we could set up a rendezvous. Then I'd need to worry about Zak and Ariel. And any other kids who were trapped in there. My mind kept spinning.

I'd noticed before how at exactly three o'clock, Damien always clattered down the steel stairs from his office dressed in his dark-blue sweat suit and running shoes, and went for a run. During this time, Elmore cleaned his office.

Today, I was watching and ready. I saw Damien do a few stretches near the stairs, then set off at a steady jog towards the main gates. Elmore came out of the laundry area, heading for the office. I saw him go inside with his cleaning gear stowed in his bucket.

I came out from around the corner where I'd been innocently dawdling and quickly followed him, checking that no one was looking before I slipped inside the building.

Elmore was whistling softly to himself and the office door was slightly ajar. I peeked in and saw him wiping Damien's desk, his back turned to me. I crept into the room, ducking down behind the long couch under the banks of security screens. I glanced up. In one of them, I could see the tall figure of Damien running across the grassy area towards the beach. Elmore wiped the large windows, picked up the wastepaper basket, emptied its contents into his bucket and mopped around the floor before taking a quick look around the room.

I crouched lower, flattening myself, as he came over to the couch. I heard him punching the cushions into shape. I held my breath. Then released it as he left the room, closing the door behind him. In a box on the bottom shelf behind the couch, I spotted a pile of stinger suits. I grabbed one, stashing it inside my jacket, hoping the bulkiness wouldn't be too obvious.

I jumped up and went straight to the key rack. I grabbed the key labeled D-2 and looked closer at the D-11 key. Next to the new label there was a tiny bit of an old tag that was still stuck to the thick string. This must be the key to Delta 11, but I still didn't know where that was. I couldn't see any other Delta keys for now.

As I turned to leave, I looked out the window and to my horror, I saw Damien running back towards the resort gates! He must have forgotten something. In my shock to be out of there, I accidently bumped one of the open laptops on the desk and it immediately flashed out of its energy-saving mode, revealing its desktop screen, full of file icons.

I stared transfixed at the top left-hand icon.

Mordred Key

The file was about the Mordred Key!
I could use the Stealth Hacker program to

find out the truth about the Mordred Key! But now wasn't the time.

I flew out of the office, skidded down the steel steps and out the door of the office building. In my haste, I crashed right into someone.

"What do you think you're doing here?" It was Dean, the counselor I'd met on my first day on the island.

"Erm, looking for Damien," I said, breathless, still wild with excitement about what I'd just discovered.

"He's not here right now," said Dean. "You shouldn't be here at all." He frowned. "And you should cut down on carbs, Ryan—you're gaining weight."

"Yep, sure thing. I'm just a bad, bad kid!" I said, trying to laugh it off. "My apologies. I'm outta here right now!"

And I jogged away, waving at Damien as he went past me with a frown on his face. I didn't look back.

My phone vibrated in my pocket—

📱 Good news bro. Found Zak!

At least he hadn't been captured along with Ariel.

I replied—

📱 Awesome! Need to swap back asap—got key to free Sophie.

His reply came back immediately—

On my way!

As soon as I was out of sight, I took off, heading for the coast. There was no way I could get back into the mountain through the secret rock face after what happened yesterday. Security would certainly be tighter now. I would have to go over the rocks all the way around to the big cavern. I took off my outer clothing and pulled the stinger suit on. The tide was coming in and the waves were high, crashing over me as I went. As if the journey wasn't already hazardous enough. A couple of times I was almost sucked under by the force of the waves, but I managed to cling on to the jagged rocks, my fingers screaming with the effort.

Mountain Bunker

4:16 pm

Finally, I got to the cavern entrance, and swam into it on a wave that surged all the way along the stone wharf. I noticed the outboard was back, roped very securely, behind the submersible.

I hauled myself out of the water and onto the rock shelf. Dripping wet, I made my way to the corridor entrance, hoping like crazy I didn't bump into anyone. All seemed quiet, but I could hear shouted orders coming from the arena area and I hoped that the Zenith team and their trainers were fully occupied for the moment. Stealthily, I hurried down the corridor and knocked on the door to D-1. No answer. I hurried to D-2, pulling the key out of my pocket, hastily knocking and turning the key at the same time.

"Sophie, it's me, Cal," I said as I pushed the door open.

"Cal! Thank goodness you're here!"

At that moment, I heard voices in the corridor, headed straight for us. I closed the door behind me, putting my finger to my lips. Sophie was silent beside me, listening. The voices got louder—one was Damien's.

"She needs to be transferred to the outcrop, to Delta 11," he said, "just in case."

Sophie looked at me uncomprehendingly. But I was beginning to understand. Damien wanted Sophie transferred to the prison on the outcrop. Brittany's desperate flight with the torn key tag in her hand and her strange words—"Help him!"—were starting to make sense. Had she been referring to the prisoner on Delta 11? The prisoner who "knows what's going on?" Was that what Damien had planned for Sophie?

A key went into the lock. Of course he would have extra keys, I realized as I threw myself under the bed. I heard the bed creak as Sophie sat on it above me, her legs and feet inches away from my face.

"Sophie, my dear," I heard Damien say from my hiding place. "I've got some good news for you."

"The only good news I want to hear from you, Damien," Sophie said, her voice angry, "is that you're letting me out. You can't keep me here like this!"

"Well, that's why I'm here. In an hour or so, we'll take you by boat to somewhere where you can be picked up easily. You'll be on your way home very soon. I'm sorry you weren't able to fit in with our happy community."

"Happy community? Are you joking? This place is run like a prison. As soon as I get home I'm going to—"

"Going to what?" Damien's voice was quiet and calm . . . and chilling.

"Nothing," said Sophie, realizing she'd already said too much.

"So, get your things ready and I'll send someone shortly to help you with your transfer. OK?"

4:34 pm

I heard the door close behind him and listened as his footsteps echoed up the corridor. I scrambled out from under the bed.

"Damien says I'm going home," Sophie said. "But that's not true, is it? I heard him say 'Delta 11'—is he planning to make me one of those missing kids?"

"Sophie," I said, "Delta 11 is a prison on that tiny island that we can see from the beach."

"There's really a prison?" she asked, her face pale with shock. "I thought those stories were just rumors."

"I went out there. I've seen it. I talked to the guy who's locked up there."

Sophie's eyes went wide.

"Look," I said, "let's get out of here and then I'll tell you everything."

Checking that the coast was clear, we stole out of Delta 2. I told Sophie about Ariel being captured. "I don't think she's locked up here," I whispered. "I knocked on the door," I said, pointing to D-1, "before I unlocked yours. There was no one there."

Silently, we fled down the corridor, out into the large cavern and along the stone ledge past the submersible, heading for the opening to the coast and the ocean. I couldn't risk staying to search for Ariel. I'd have to come back for her.

I gave Sophie the stinger suit to wear, praying that the jellies would keep out of this crashing surf. I knew they were more likely in quieter waters, but that was no guarantee. The tide was even higher now and a couple of times we had to cling on in order not to be swept away.

Halfway to shore, Sophie lost her footing and I grabbed her wrist tight, as we struggled not to be swept out to sea. The swell was getting bigger with each passing minute.

Finally, exhausted, we made it to shore and headed inland near the resort compound.

"I've got somewhere safe to take you," I said, "if I can ever find it again." I was thinking of Ariel and Zak's cave where, hopefully, Zak would be waiting. If they'd managed to stay hidden for months, chances were that Sophie would be safe there too until we could make our escape from the island.

We were both weary and wringing wet, but we forced ourselves to start climbing towards the rainforest. I realized I didn't know exactly where Zak and Ariel's comfortable cave was, and I knew I had to get the key back before I was missed.

But when they came back to get Sophie and found her missing, the whole place would be in an uproar. Not even those problems could take away the excitement I was feeling underneath everything else. At last I had some way of discovering what the Mordred Key was all about.

I couldn't wait to get back into Damien's office with the Stealth Hacker!

Painfully slowly, we made our way through dense jungle. I was parting some heavy vines when I saw a movement ahead—something creeping stealthily a few yards away. I put my arm out to stop Sophie from taking another step and as I did so, someone pounced on me, knocking me down. I scrambled to get up.

A figure loomed over me, with a bow and arrow. I heard Sophie's sharp intake of breath.

"Zak?" I hissed.

"Cal?"

"Nice take-down, Zak," I said, getting to my feet, brushing the mud off my knees. Zak put his bow and arrow down.

"Sorry," he said.

"OK, you two," said Sophie, startled. "What's going on?"

Katz Cave

5:35 pm

We filled Sophie in as Zak led us back to his cave. At the end of his story, his face was etched with concern for his sister.

"So how did Ariel get caught?" I asked.

"We followed you into the mountain as planned

and gave you a few minutes to find Sophie," Zak said. "We knocked over some equipment in that big cavern to distract everyone, then ran for it. We were almost outside when someone grabbed Ariel. Before I could go back in, she kicked the branch out of the way so the door would close. Crazy girl!"

"*Brave* girl," said Sophie. "Thank you," she added quietly.

"I searched the mountain corridor for Ariel. I'm sorry, I don't know where she is. But don't worry, Zak, I promise I'll help you find her," I said, as we went through the well-camouflaged opening to the cave.

Zak's face paled, then he gave a small smile, "Thanks, Cal, I know you will."

Then I told Sophie more about my night journey to the outcrop. "There's a guy there, locked up in a cement bunker. He asked me to help him, but when I asked him who he was, he couldn't tell me."

"What do you mean, *couldn't* tell you?" asked Sophie, pushing wet hair back from her face, wrapping herself in the sarong that Zak gave her.

"He literally didn't know who he was. I couldn't get any sense out of him. He only seemed able to say two things: 'Help me' and 'I don't know.' His voice sounded—rusty."

My phone chimed and I grabbed it. It was a text from Winter. I read it out.

📱 Meanings for Mordred . . . a character from King Arthur. Treacherous, traitor to the king. A close relative, but while Arthur's away, Mordred rebels. Tries to take over kingdom. Mordred = rebellion against rightful authority. Aka a destructive force. Hope that helps! Wx

So a Mordred Key might be connected to taking over something or someone and trying to replace it or them. Didn't ring any bells for me.

"Do you think the Mordred Key is something to do with Delta 11?" Sophie asked. "That's the most secret place around here. That would be the place to keep something hidden."

"Your guess is as good as mine," I said. "But I'm hoping to get more information very soon," I said, describing my visit to Damien's office and what I'd seen on his screen. "Maybe Mordred is about replacing something legitimate with something bad."

Zak frowned. "That could mean a lot of things," he said.

"It could," I agreed. "But it's a start. And if I can get hold of whatever's on Damien's computer, we might find out a whole lot more."

With a stick, I did a sketch of the sword with the serpent wound around it on the sandy floor of the cave. "This is what the icon for the Mordred Key looked like."

"Swords and snakes," said Sophie. "Not crazy about either of those."

"Sophie," I said, looking up from the drawing, thinking of Winter and Boges. "You really could be more helpful back on the mainland. I know my friends Winter and Boges would like you. You could be a member of the team. You're in constant danger here and—" I was cut off by the sounds of people yelling and shouting.

"What's that?" Zak asked.

Down at the resort, the loudspeakers blared.

6:01 pm

At first I thought Sophie's absence from Delta 2 had been discovered, but a loud noise outside the cave had us all on our feet ready to bolt.

Someone was coming straight for the cave!

Before we could take any action, the cave's narrow entrance between the leaves darkened as a figure approached.

Ariel!

"I escaped!" she cried, as she dived inside. "They had me locked up in one of the storerooms in the mountain, but when they went in to check that I was still there, I was ready for them and took them by surprise!"

"Thank goodness you're safe!" said her brother, hugging her tightly. "I was so worried about you. We were going to rescue you!"

"Well, I've saved you the trouble! Really, I'm fine, don't worry. But I'm scared I might have brought the search party here," she said.

"We should split up," I said. "If the cave is discovered, we'll be trapped like rats and they'll catch us all. We'll meet back here later when it's safe." Within seconds, we'd scattered in different directions, taking cover wherever we could find it.

I crawled into a narrow space between a huge rotting tree trunk and a vine-covered rock, hoping my friends had found good hiding spots.

The searchers came closer. Now I could hear their words clearly as they called out to each other.

"She can't have gone far. Fan out more."

"Watch out for the Gympies!"

I sensed someone walking close to my hideout. Out of my peripheral vision, I could see sneakers moving through the leaves. All he needed to do was take two steps in my direction and he'd tread on me! I willed myself to shrink even more.

The shoes moved away and I let out a silent sigh of relief. But then came another pair, even closer. This time it was Damien. "Have you found anything, Chloe?"

"There are some broken leaves here," I heard her reply. "Someone's passed by recently."

From higher up the mountain, somebody yelled and I was very grateful to hear them because the next thing Chloe said was, "Must have been those guys up there. We should join them and see if they've found anything."

Ten minutes later, all was still. The search party had gone high up the mountain. I waited another five minutes and then, moving with great stealth, I crawled out of my hiding place. Everything was quiet. Movement nearby made me start in fright. Then a voice. "It's OK, Cal. It's me. And Ariel. We dug under this boulder ages ago in case we needed a bolt-hole."

I watched as Zak and Ariel brushed mud and leaves off their arms.

"Where's Sophie?" I asked.

Zak and Ariel looked at each other. "Maybe she's already back at the cave?"

But when we got back, there was no sign of her. I wasn't sure what to do. Should I risk going out to look for her, or wait for her to come to us? I was trying to decide when a noise made us all jump.

The radio had sprung into life! For the first time ever, SI-6 was calling me.

Zak looked on, startled.

"I'll explain everything, I promise," I said as I grabbed the radio out of its hiding place.

"Night Hawk, this is Condor. Copy please."

"Condor, this is Night Hawk. So relieved to hear from you. We've been having difficulties making contact with you."

"That's why I'm calling, Night Hawk. We hadn't heard from you for a while. Do you read . . . copy . . ." The line was dropping out again.

"Condor? Do you read me?" I tried in vain. There was only static.

I swung around at a different sound behind me. Sophie Bellamy stood there, her pretty freckled face pulled into a scowl. "What's going on? That was my father's voice! You're talking to *my father?*"

Sophie wasn't supposed to find out like this. "Sophie, listen," I started to say.

But she wasn't listening. Her face screwed up in fury. "You're working for my *father! He* sent you. You've been spying on me all this time. How could you? You lied to me! I *trusted* you!"

"Sophie, *please*. It's not like that, I promise."

She didn't want to hear it, instead she continued shouting. "Pretending to be my friend and all the time reporting on me back to my father? You had no right to do that!"

"Just listen to me, will you?"

But flinging me a last, furious look, she turned and crashed through the tangle of leaves and vines and out of the cave.

I took off after her. "Sophie! Come back. It's not like that! Please, you've got it all wrong. Come back and let's talk about it!"

I could hear her ahead of me, smashing her way through the rainforest.

"Come back! It might not be safe!"

My words had no effect. The way she was going, she would run straight-bang into the arms of the search party. I had to stop her, for her own sake.

Overhead, thunder grumbled and the sky darkened.

Shadow Island Jungle

6:38 pm

The thunder rolled overhead as the storm front grew closer. How was I going to get out of this mess? Sophie *had* to get off the island now. The search would be relentless because she knew too much. Unlike other kids who might have run away from the resort compound, Sophie had been right into the heart of the mountain, where the secret training area lay. Damien *had* to silence her. This was serious.

Lower down I could hear search parties making another pass over the foothills.

"Spread out and search every inch of your area," I heard Damien ordering through a bullhorn.

Zak had suddenly joined me. I hadn't heard him coming at all. "Cal, we have to find her," he said, his suntanned face tight with fear and concern.

"Zak's right," said Ariel, who had materialized behind her brother.

This wasn't working, I thought, randomly searching, exposing ourselves to capture. We needed to think of a plan.

"We'll go back to your cave," I said. "They haven't ever found that. We'll be safe there for a while. We can plan what we're going to do next. Let's hope Sophie stays well-hidden."

I sounded confident, but I wasn't.

We made our way back through the rainforest as quickly as we dared, trying not to leave obvious footprints or broken vines behind us. All the time, my head was whirling, trying to come up with a plan that would work. It had to be a big plan. I had to find Sophie, get into Damien's office with the Stealth Hacker, send the data to SI-6 and Boges, make sure Ryan was OK and free the unknown prisoner from Delta 11.

I could just hear Boges saying, "Sure, dude. Should be easy as!"

We squeezed through the well-hidden entry to the cave, rearranging the thick greenery behind us. I knew I wasn't the only person holding my breath as I crouched down with Zak and Ariel.

Katz Cave

7:02 pm

They came close again, slashing through the vines and muttering about the obstacles. A moment later, I heard Dean. He was standing just outside the concealed entrance.

"She's somewhere on this island and we have plenty of searchers. You all go up that way again—" I imagined him pointing "—and you all, head up over there. I'll take a look around here and then join you."

I was too scared to risk even a peep through the leaves. Instead I huddled together with the others.

Finally, the noises died down as the search party moved away.

The rainforest had been quiet for some time. There was just the steady sound of the rain and the slapping of palm leaves in the wind.

"I think they've gone," I whispered. "At least for now."

"We've got to find Sophie," said Ariel, her brown eyes concerned.

Before anyone could even move, there was a sound outside. We froze at the noise. It came again. I looked out, scared and anxious. Not far from the cave, something was moving in the undergrowth. Cautiously, I peered through some leafy cover to see a python heading our way.

"It's a snake," I said, stepping through the cave's leafy entrance, and watching, waiting for it to cross the open area ahead of me and disappear again into the thick undergrowth. But it didn't. It turned and now it was heading straight at me. I jumped sideways calling as loudly as I dared to the others. "Look out!"

The creature sidled closer. I'd read in a nature magazine that snakes are timid animals and prefer to get out of the way of any threat rather than fight it. This snake hadn't read the magazine. It seemed to be intent on coming straight towards me, and when I moved sideways, it did the same. It came closer, rearing up. Quick as a flash, I picked up a heavy branch and hit it. I'd only meant to discourage it, but the blow had been harder than I intended and now the creature lay on the rainforest floor, the back half wiggling, the front half still. I looked closer.

"Geez!" said Zak, taking the words right out of my mouth.

"Oh my goodness!" cried Ariel. "What on earth is *that?*"

I stood there staring at what lay on the path. This was no snake. Inside the torn skin, I could see wiring, circuitry and electronic components.

"It's man-made!" Zak said. "Those pythons aren't real. They're some kind of robot!"

In front of our eyes, the electronic snake started to twist and heave. We watched in amazement as the undamaged remainder of its body regrouped, leaving the damaged section on the forest floor. Then, slightly shorter than it had been, the robot python slid away. Just before it vanished, I came out of my stunned state and managed to get a picture of it on my phone.

Shadow Island had suddenly hit a new level of weird. Before we had a chance to talk about what we'd just seen, I froze again. It was a clap of thunder accompanying a sudden heavy shower, but over the noise of the rain, I could hear someone calling my name.

Zak put his hand on my arm. "Careful, it could be a trap. It could be anything after what we've just seen!" Zak had a point. My mind raced to process this new threat. No one here knew my name except Zak, Ariel, Ryan and Sophie. Zak and Ariel were with me, Ryan was down at the resort, so it had to be . . .

"Sophie?" I called softly.

Sophie Bellamy stood there, rain running down her face, scratches on her arms and legs from her wild run into the jungle. Her eyes were red and I knew she'd been crying. I went to her, putting the crazy snake out of my mind for the time being.

"Sophie, I'm so sorry you had to find out about me and your father in that way. I was going to tell you at the right moment. But thank goodness you're safe."

She flashed a glance at me and I could see that she was still angry with me.

"If you'd just let me explain. Come inside, quick. Everybody on the island is out looking for you."

Inside, Zak passed her a towel and she rubbed her face and arms, finally squatting down beside us. "I came back because I realized I don't really have anywhere else to go. I'm not saying I forgive you, but I will listen to what you have to say." A frown lined her forehead again. "I'm warning you, it better be good."

"It is, I promise." I decided to tell her everything

from the very beginning. "I'm probably breaking the Official Secrets Act," I said, "but because you're part of the family, I'm hoping it won't go too hard for me."

I really had her interest now. So I told her how I'd been set up by SI-6, the frightening tests I'd been put through, BB telling me about his concerns for Sophie's whereabouts and safety. "He didn't ask me to spy on you, or tell on you. No way. All he wanted to know was that if you were here, that you were safe. That was my mission. And at the same time, your father wanted me to have a look around the Paradise People Resort—get an idea of what sort of a place it was, and if Damien was running the place well. Once I'd done that, I was to come back to the mainland. That's it."

Sophie looked up at me with her big blue eyes. "I know Dad means well. He always says he's only got my best interests at heart and I'm sure that's true. But he is so hard on me. Because of the sort of work he does, he always thinks the worst is going to happen. He used to have security guys follow me to school. It drove me nuts. I felt like a prisoner. It's much easier when I stay with Mum, but she's away a lot because of her work. Dad and I had this big fight one night and I took off. I miss Dad and I love him, but I can't live like that any longer."

As I listened to Sophie, all I could think of was how lucky she was to have her father, but I kept that thought to myself.

"Sophie," I said, "that must have been tough. But please believe that I was going to go back to the mainland after checking that you were OK. It's only since discovering that something bad is happening here that my plans have changed. We really should get off the island as soon as possible."

"But what about the other kids? What about the man on Delta 11?" Sophie said.

"BB and SI-6 will figure that out. He might want me to come back or they might send their own guys."

"And Sophie," Ariel said, "you'll never believe what just happened."

"With all the weird things happening in this place, I doubt you could surprise me."

We told her about the python and she blinked. "OK. I take it back, I'm surprised," she said. "Robot pythons that repair themselves? Who made them? What do they do?"

"That's what I'm here for," I said, sending the photo of the python to Boges. "That's why your father sent me here. I sure have some things to tell him." What was this place, I thought, that looked like a dream vacation resort and turned out to be more like a secret commando center? What sort of a place has "snakebots?"

"Quiet! Someone's coming!" Zak had jumped up and was peering through a tiny crack in the leaves. "You're not going to believe this," he hissed, "but Damien is headed right this way—with Hamish!"

My phone started chiming—Ryan. I banged it quiet. Had Damien and Hamish heard that?

Slowly, I stood up to join Zak, nudging a branch to catch a glimpse of the two of them deep in discussion. Damien had his back to us, but I could clearly see the grimace on Hamish's face. As we watched, they slowly turned and started pushing their way through the undergrowth, going higher up through the rainforest, faces determined, looking for Sophie.

"Can I stay here for a while, please?" Sophie whispered.

"Of course," said Ariel.

"Awesome!" I said, glancing at the text that Ryan had sent me. I showed the others—

▊ Got master key to office.

I fired right back.

▊ Great work, bro. How?

Ryan replied.

▊ Elmore left keys on verandah. Grabbed master. Hidden in my mattress, inside comic. Damien grounded me for going out of bounds.

But forget that. I'm on my way to find you.

No, I thought. I texted.

📱 Stay there! I'm on my way to swap places.

📱 Too late. Already halfway to you bro. You're not the only daredevil in this family.

This was bad. Sometimes Ryan didn't think things through. What if we ran into each other on the mountain and the searchers saw us together? We could both end up on Delta 11. I tried texting again, but Ryan had switched off his phone, keeping out of sight as he made his way here.

I couldn't worry about that right now because a plan was forming in my mind.

"Gotta go, guys. This is the sort of chance you only get once. Damien is up here in the jungle. I'm going to be down there in his office! Tell Ryan to wait here, I won't be long." I checked my pocket, making sure that the Stealth Hacker was tucked in there.

I took off down the mountain, making sure I kept out of sight. I could hear the search parties still calling to each other, their voices echoing higher up on the mountain. I skidded and slid in the freshly wet soil. The rain had eased although the wind was becoming stronger.

I emerged through the cemetery, heading for the big mango and palm trees near the kayaks, staying back until I'd scoped out the resort. The palm trees that fringed the beach bent and waved in the wind.

Paradise People Resort

7:57 pm

It looked like everyone was still out searching because there were no counselors on duty and the compound gates were partly open. Only Elmore, standing on the verandah of the dining room, was visible. I sidled around the boys' dormitory, taking cover in between the clotheslines and the dripping-wet sheets that were hanging there. As I skirted around some buildings, I could hear a bunch of kids at the beach—laughing and messing around, oblivious to the drama unfolding in the jungle.

I bolted into the dormitory, straight to Ryan's bed, lifting up the mattress. Sure enough, there was a superhero comic and inside that— the master key! I was concerned about Ryan's whereabouts right now, but I had to hand it to the guy. This was a major, major coup.

Doubling over, I scrambled across the empty space between the dormitories. I did my best to avoid the CCTV areas, but I knew I'd have to go past one of them to get into the office. I pulled my hoodie right up over my face and kept my head down. I skidded up the few steps into the office building and clanged up the steel stairs to the locked door. I pulled out the master key, and the lock turned smoothly. Closing the door behind me, I took a step into the room. On the CCTV monitor screens, I could see the deserted compound and Elmore pulling his cart over towards the recreation center. Somewhere in the distance, I could hear yelling and shouting. Stay focused, I thought, hurrying over to Damien's desk.

The two laptops sat there, their lids open. Only one appeared to be switched on—the laptop with the desktop icons showing. Anxiously I scanned them. One called Robotics and another named Electronic Engineering grabbed my interest, but there was only one I could afford to focus on right now. There it was! The Mordred Key icon.

I was about to click on it and open it when something else on the screen caught my eye. At first I thought it was identical to the mysterious image texted to me a few weeks ago. The world map and the superimposed skull and crossbones were there, but something was different—instead of "90 days," there was a digital clock ticking over, counting down days, hours, minutes and seconds. It was currently at sixty days.

Sixty days until what?

I took a quick picture of it with my phone then tore myself away from trying to figure it out and clicked on the Mordred Key icon.

It opened, but I couldn't make sense of what I was looking at—a mess of data, letters, what I thought might be Greek and Russian script, signs, occasional scraps of words, figures—it looked like total junk—and there were pages and pages of it. What could it mean? I pulled the Stealth Hacker out of my pocket. Pushing it into a port, I tried to start the download. The download bar appeared, but nothing seemed to be happening.

8:12 pm

Outside, voices were coming. On the TV screen, I could see Damien at the head of the pack of people on their way back to the resort. I prayed they hadn't found Sophie. Maybe she'd given herself up to save Zak's hide-out.

The download bar began filling very, very slowly—12% . . . 18% . . . 21% . . .

"Come *on. Hurry up!*"

27% . . .

I couldn't believe the slow download.

To ease my anxiety, I minimized the file, and

checked out the other icons on the desktop. There were various files, for the CCTV, attendance lists, amenities, advertising material and another icon labeled "Emergency."

Outside the noise had become really loud and I flattened myself against the wall to peer out one of the floor-to-ceiling glass windows. To my horror I saw that Damien was striding across the compound, already through the gates, dragging a struggling figure. From this distance, I couldn't see who it was.

43 . . . 54% . . . 61% . . .

Hurry, *hurry.*

The group and the struggling captive came into view. I groaned. My worst fear had been realized. The struggling figure was my brother, Ryan.

Ryan had obviously been caught during the search for Sophie and was now being hauled back by a very angry Damien, and worse still, I knew he would be brought up here into the office. I could hear Ryan yelling out as Damien, now with Dean's assistance, manhandled him across the wide sports field heading for the office building. Thank you, Ryan, I thought, as I realized he was making all that noise to make sure I knew they were coming. So I could get out . . . but I was stuck. Behind them, the staff who'd been in the search parties peeled off to their various dormitories and to the recreation center.

73% . . . 85% . . .

The download was taking forever to finish. I couldn't leave yet.

Finally, it finished, but that was only the first part. The Stealth Hacker had two parts, and the second was just as important—Cover Tracks.

Thank goodness that program was much faster. My pulse was racing, the blood pounding in my head. It was still taking way too long. Slow seconds ticked by and then it was done. Frantically, I whipped out the USB from the port, loading it into my phone. I emailed it to BB as the commotion outside the office building got louder. With fumbling fingers, I emailed it to Boges as well.

I just had time to close down the Mordred Key program as I heard them starting up the stairs. But where could I go? Where could I hide? I looked around the room, realizing the couch would not suffice this time. My heart sank.

There was no way out.

As the footsteps rang out on the steel stairway, and my brother's struggles failed to stop their progress, I desperately spun around, looking for an escape.

Any second now and they'd be through the door and into Damien's office. Ryan and I would come face to face and Damien would discover our secret. I thought of Damien's chilling tone earlier and shivered. He would be furious. What would happen to us after that was anybody's guess.

But I knew it couldn't be good.

4S RACE AGAINST TIME 06:48 07:12 05:21 RACE AGAI
ICE AGAINST TIME SEEK THE TRUTH . . . CONSPIRACY
ONE SOMETHING IS SERIOUSLY MESSED UP HERE 0:
:07 06:06 06:07 MISSING WHO CAN CAL TRUST? SEE
:05 MISSING 06:04 10:08 RACE AGAINST TIME 02:27
EEK THE TRUTH 01:00 07:57 SOMETHING IS SERIOUSL
ERE 05:01 09:53 CONSPIRACY 365 12:00 RACE AGAIN!
:17 MISSING WHO CAN CAL TRUST? 01:09 LET THE CO
EGIN MISSING HIDING SOMETHING? 03:32 01:47 05:03
T THE COUNTDOWN BEGIN 09:06 10:33 11:45 RACE A!
:48 07:12 05:21 RACE AGAINST TIME RACE AGAINST
IE TRUTH . . . CONSPIRACY 365 TRUST NO ONE 06:07
SERIOUSLY MESSED UP HERE 08:30 12:01 05:07 06:
SSING WHO CAN CAL TRUST? SEEK THE TRUTH 12:0!
:04 10:08 RACE AGAINST TIME 02:27 08:06 10:32 SE
:00 7:57 SOMETHING IS SERIOUSLY MESSED UP HER
NSPIRACY 365 12:00 RACE AGAINST TIME 04:31 10:
N CAL TRUST? 01:09 LET THE COUNTDOWN BEGIN M
METHING? 03:32 01:47 05:03 MISSING LET THE COL
EGIN 09:06 10:33 11:45 RACE AGAINST TIME 06:48 07
AINST TIME RACE AGAINST TIME SEEK THE TRUTH .
5 TRUST NO ONE SOMETHING IS 06:07 SERIOUSLY (
ERE 08:30 12:01 05:07 06:06 06:07 MISSING WHO CA.
EK THE TRUTH 12:03 MISSING 06:04 10:08 RACE AG
:27 08:06 10:32 SEEK THE TRUTH 01:00 07:57 SOM!
ERIOUSLY MESSED UP HERE 05:01 09:53 CONSPIRAC
CE AGAINST TIME 04:31 10:17 MISSING WHO CAN CA
T THE COUNTDOWN BEGIN MISSING HIDING SOMETH
:47 05:03 MISSING LET THE COUNTDOWN BEGIN 09:
CE AGAINST TIME 06:48 07:12 05:21 RACE AGAINST
AINST TIME SEEK THE TRUTH . . . CONSPIRACY 365
METHING IS 06:07 SERIOUSLY MESSED UP HERE O
:07 06:06 06:07 MISSING WHO CAN CAL TRUST? SE
:05 MISSING 06:04 10:08 RACE AGAINST TIME 02:2
EK THE TRUTH 01:00 07:57 SOMETHING IS SERIOUS